LETTERS FOR PHOEBE

Letters FOR Phoebe

FOREVER AFTER

SALLY BRITTON

Sally Britton
www.authorsallybritton.com

First Printing: July 2020

To Joanna, Megan, Heidi, and Rachel:
I'm forever grateful that we met.

PROLOGUE

SURREY, ENGLAND, 1808

P hoebe Kimball tied the last of the sticky treats in a handkerchief, already questioning if it was wise to nip the Chelsea buns from the kitchen instead of the much less messy ginger biscuits. But tonight was not about avoiding messes. It was about bidding farewell to one of her dearest friends. While Phoebe liked most of the girls at school well enough, there were four she considered as close to her as sisters.

She gathered up the buns and picked her way back through the kitchen, around work tables, to the doorway where Daphne waited. She nearly giggled at the way her friend stood, as rigid as a soldier on watch for an enemy.

"Hurry, Phoebe," Daphne whispered.

Phoebe stepped directly next to her friend as she spoke. "Already done."

Daphne jumped. Truly, Phoebe's friend was not one to break the rules. Sneaking out to meet their friends already made her nervous, but *borrowing* things from the kitchen had stretched her.

Phoebe offered what she hoped was a reassuring grin.

"How many times have we done this, and still you are nervous?" She turned to lead the way to the back door. She barely heard Daphne's step behind her. They knew well enough which floorboards to avoid. They had been at Mrs. Vernal's Seminary for Distinguished Young Ladies for *years*.

"Not nervous," Daphne answered. "Just appropriately cautious."

Phoebe had to swallow a giggle. "Of course."

Though amused in the moment, Phoebe had depended upon Daphne's good sense and caution on more than one occasion. While Phoebe considered herself a planner, she sometimes forgot to keep herself within the bounds of propriety when working toward her goals.

The lawn stretched before them, the moonlight showing the way as clear, though the shadows of trees and shrubs remained black. She shivered, though it was not too cold for an April night.

When they came near the gazebo, she could hear Marah and Isabel's quiet voices. Good. They had already arrived. Her heart dropped as she and Daphne went to the steps. Phoebe didn't want this to be their last time together, but Marah had to leave. She hadn't expected to lose practical Marah first. She was so young, but word of her father's death had come as well as a summons to return home.

Phoebe swallowed back her hurt on behalf of her friend when she heard Isabel's voice, snapping her attention back to the present.

"I know what might help," Isabel said to Marah, beckoning Daphne and Phoebe to her. "Your best friends with your favorite—"

"Chelsea buns!" Phoebe forced a bright smile,

knowing they could see her expression well enough as she held up her package of smushed sweets.

"Phoebe, Daphne," Marah said suspiciously. "You didn't make those, did you?"

"We didn't make them." Phoebe's smile settled to something more natural. Tonight was about giving Marah a proper send-off. She had to remember that. "We *borrowed* them from the kitchen."

Daphne sounded more amused than disapproving when she spoke. "Yes, and I do not think they'll want them back after what Phoebe's done to them."

Isabel laughed, but Marah only shook her head. "You shouldn't have taken them. The last time Phoebe stole from the kitchens, she had to teach the first years how to sip their tea correctly. I don't want you to—"

Daphne stepped forward, laying a gentle hand on Marah's arm. "You're leaving tomorrow, Marah. You needn't worry about us."

Though Phoebe could have done without the reminder of her punishment, she shrugged off the concern. Then she looked about the gazebo. They were missing someone rather important. "Where is Lavinia? It's not like her to call a meeting and then be the last to show."

A stern voice came behind them, mimicking their headmistress. "I won't begin until everyone is sitting quietly with their hands in the laps and their eyes on me." Lavinia stepped up onto the gazebo with her nose in the air, hands clasped neatly before her in the spitting image of the stern proprietress of the school.

"Who invited Mrs. Vernal?" Isabel asked, voice dripping with disapproval.

Lavinia laughed, breaking her act and coming to

join the other girls. "I've a surprise for you. When have you ever known Mrs. Vernal to say that?"

Phoebe winced. "Once. Before the Latin test." The Latin test Phoebe had failed rather miserably.

The girls giggled as they settled onto the blankets spread on the wooden planks of the gazebo. Phoebe settled the snacks next to her, safely wrapped in her hand-kerchiefs. The laundry maid would not thank Phoebe for the extra sticky linens to clean.

Lavinia pulled a small sack from behind her back and set it before her. "Under normal circumstances, you know I would say we should eat first. But tonight, the food can wait."

With her mind upon the food, Phoebe's complaint slipped out without thought. "Must it, though? I'm near to starving."

"Her stomach was growling all the way here," Daphne confirmed.

Phoebe sent her a mock glare as the girls laughed again, and Daphne returned it with a sly grin. Teasing each other came naturally with these dear friends. Sometimes, Phoebe pretended they really were sisters. Their bond had to be nearly as strong as one of blood, given how much they had been through together since meeting.

Isabel held up a brown leather book. "Or, better than Chelsea buns, we could discover what happens at the end of *The Love of Count Rudolph* by Eugenia Rutherfield."

Before Phoebe could petition to begin with their treat again, Marah let out an audible groan.

Isabel pointed the corner of the book at her. "But we only have one night left together! Come, Marah, you must be the slightest bit curious to know if the Count will save Lady Esmerelda."

"That isn't how life goes, you know." Marah spoke with an ever-so-practical tilt of her head. "The handsome gentleman doesn't parade in on his white horse to save the lady from all her troubles."

"Isn't it nice to imagine, though?" Daphne said, leaning toward Marah with a suggestive raise to her eyebrow. "When the count saved Lady Esmerelda from the evil baron, I practically swooned."

Marah lips twitched, but then Isabel spoke. "I think she will save herself in the end. We don't need men to save us from everything, you know." Isabel's voice always grew a bit louder when she spoke of things she was passionate about, and now was no exception. Though Phoebe often agreed with her friend's rather progressive views for the fair sex, she stayed out of the argument.

Lavinia made a sound of exasperation. "You girls have the attention span of a…a…" she threw up her hands. "A senile goose. I brought a surprise, remember?"

Phoebe bit her lip, darting a glance around quickly enough to know how they must respond. "Yes, Mrs. Vernal," she said with her friends, then they all burst out laughing.

"Oh, hush." But even Lavinia grinned at them. She was something of a mother-hen, forever bringing them to attention even if amused by their inability to sit still. "I've been sad about Marah leaving. And Isabel and I only have a few more weeks before we're done with school. Soon we'll be separated."

That sobered all of them, and Phoebe felt her smile fade away as her eyes went first to Marah and then her other friends. She and Daphne would be the last two to leave the school. It was the end of an era, the end of child-hood. She hated to let them go with a fierceness that made her chest tighten and her eyes burn.

Life would never be the same again.

"I was in Marlow's shop today," Lavinia went on, her voice softer, "and I saw the absolute most perfect thing that made me think of all of you." She took out a beaded bracelet. "It reminds me of all our good times. I thought we could send it with Marah, so she'll take a part of us with her."

A truly marvelous thought, but before Phoebe could say so, Marah was already shaking her head. "No, I couldn't. It's far too expensive."

Phoebe leaned forward, trying to convey what she felt in her eyes and voice. "But you are facing hardship at this moment. Why not keep it for now, and perhaps later you might send it to one of us? Should we need comforting. It could bring you luck." Not that Phoebe particularly believed in luck. But she did believe in her friends.

"Yes, I love it." Lavinia smiled. "We can send it on to one another. It will keep us connected."

Daphne's soft voice was the next to offer reassur-ance. "Like the locket Count Rudolph gave to Esmerelda, when he promised to always love her."

Phoebe darted a surprised glance at her friend. She hadn't thought Daphne was as enamored by the romance as Phoebe was. True, the gothic novel had more than one silly passage that made them giggle, but at the heart of the story was the love between the count and his Esmerelda. A love story that defied the odds, leaping over every obstacle in its path. The reality of English romance and marriage was far removed from the story they had read aloud to each other for weeks. The reality was likely that Phoebe would be introduced to some stuffy gentleman at a ball who might take enough of a liking to her to send her flowers the next day.

How dull.

Marah snorted at Daphne's words, but Isabel only squeezed an arm around her shoulder. "I will always love you, Marah. And you, Mrs. Vernal."

Lavinia laughed, but Phoebe's mind grew serious as she turned about her thoughts of the future. What if their future could have romance in it? Something more than the cold formality of a Society courtship?

"As foolish as we are behaving now," she said, "it would mean a great deal to me to know each of you finds a love like that. I cannot like the idea of any of you marrying someone who does not treasure you." Someone who would only see their dowries, or their pretty faces. Each of her friends deserved a husband who would see their goodness and their hearts.

Lavinia took up the idea with an eager nod. "We should make a pact. A promise. To marry for love." Phoebe held her breath, looking to the others. She hadn't expected Lavinia to take up the idea so quickly.

"To marry only for the truest love," Daphne said into the quiet that had settled upon their gazebo. "A love that withstands every challenge and trial."

Isabel's eyes grew serious. "To men who treat us as equals."

"Who can make us laugh even on the worst of days," Phoebe added, some of the heaviness lifting from her heart.

"Who would stop at nothing to win our hearts," came Lavinia's soft voice.

Phoebe turned her gaze to Marah, as they all did. Marah only stared at her feet. "Love is a luxury some cannot afford."

Lavinia, ever kind and nurturing, took Marah's hand. "Come, Marah, we are dreaming right now. Tell us what you want in a man."

Marah hesitated a moment longer then let out a long breath. "If I could have a man who sees me not for my economic value, but simply for me, I think I should be happy."

A lump formed in Phoebe's throat. She looked around the circle of girls, meeting their eyes in turn. "We must promise to *try*."

Lavinia held out the bracelet, the red beads a glimmering circle in her palm, reflecting the weak moon-light. Daphne reached out first and touched the bracelet, Isabel's and Phoebe's hands following soon after. Her eyes prickled, and she raised her head to look at Marah, watching them.

"All of us," Daphne said gently.

Marah sighed, then scooted forward to touch a tentative finger on the bracelet.

"A pact for love," Isabel said, "for each other, and the men we choose to stand beside us."

They nodded together, the solemnity of the moment settling heavy in the air around them.

This could not be the end. Phoebe could not accept that this would be the last time she met with her friends, speaking their secrets into the night. Somehow, they would come together again. A bond such as theirs would not be easily forgotten, nor dimmed by time.

"Give me your hand, Marah," Lavinia said, and

they all sat back save for Marah. Lavinia slipped the bracelet around her wrist, securing the gold fastener.

Phoebe had to busy herself with something else before she cried. She uncovered the Chelsea buns and Marah smiled for the first time that night as they laughed, their hands becoming sticky messes as they ate their stolen treats. Even if Cook found out, even if Phoebe had to help first years practice their German vowels for a week, it would be worth it for that shared moment of happiness.

As they settled back onto the blankets, Isabel once again held up their prized leather book. "Huddle close, ladies. *The Love of Count Rudolph*, the final chapter."

Lavinia put an arm around Marah, and Phoebe scooted closer to Daphne, wrapping a spare blanket about both their shoulders. They watched Isabel expectantly as she opened the book and paused dramatically.

"The clouds over Mount Morocco made the silvery moon seem like a ghost, and Esmerelda heard the howl of the wolf pack from a far off and shivered. Where was her handsome Count? Would he come for her? She fingered the battered locket at her chest. He'd promised his love would stretch across oceans. Was a mountain too far?"

CHAPTER 1

APRIL 1, 1812

The crowd at the park had reached ridiculous proportions, which kept Phoebe seated squarely in her small phaeton. Her driver sat stiffly before her, knowing well enough that to show interest in the display to the left of the path would not elevate him in the eyes of his mistress.

For her part, Phoebe Kimball kept her eyes averted from the ridiculous activity nearby and upon a cloud drifting overhead. She most certainly did not peer from the corner of her eye to see the two men on the green, stripped of their coats, hats, and gloves, hurling balls of dough at one another. Not like her sister-in-law, who watched the whole thing with a delicately crafted opera spyglass pressed to her eye.

A spyglass. In broad daylight.

Phoebe pushed a dark lock of hair behind her ear and made a mental note to tell her maid to use more egg-whites in her next hair-setting tonic.

Laughter erupted from the field. How two grown men, with family names well known and respected throughout

England, could behave in such a common manner, she would never know. The crowd enjoyed their well-advertised "duel," if the cheers and applause were any indication of their thoughts on the matter.

"Why they chose the fashionable hour is beyond my understanding," Phoebe muttered aloud at last. She had come hoping for a glimpse of a particularly suitable bachelor known to ride at that time. "Though the date makes perfect sense. They are behaving as fools, and they are causing a standstill on Rotten Row. This will be in all the papers."

"Of course. April is the month of fools." Caroline murmured her agreement but made no effort to ignore the fight. "Oh, the viscount lobbed that one directly into Mr. Fenwick's face. That must be the final blow. I cannot see how one might do better."

"It pains me to know you are acquainted with that man." Phoebe squeezed her eyes shut. Where did they even get all the dough for this incredible foolishness? Stolen from some overworked baker, no doubt.

There had been a time when Phoebe would have been as delighted by the spectacle as her sister-in-law. A time before her mother grew ill, before her father grew distant. Indeed, she had planned her own amusing adventures with her friends at school down to the smallest detail to ensure their merriment.

But those days were past, and Phoebe had other things to plan. Such as a marriage wherein she might be seen as an equal rather than a sack of coins. She shivered despite the sunshine pouring through the trees above.

"Oh. It is over." Caroline sat back in her seat and collapsed her telescope, her bottom lip protruding as though she had been robbed of a treat. Really. A woman of her delicate condition, even if said condition wasn't yet widely known, ought to show more decorum. "That was the liveliest thing that has happened all week."

"But hardly appropriate." Phoebe turned her head barely enough to see the crowd dispersing, but the two men in the middle of the odd display were pulling on their coats and exchanging huge grins. Phoebe hastily looked away again. "Did you hear how it came about? They were tossing food at one another at their club, like common ruffians in a public house."

Caroline had obviously grown used to Phoebe's ways and tended to ignore her sister-in-law when Phoebe addressed subjects relating to decorum. As a married woman, perhaps Caroline did not worry as much over her reputation as Phoebe must. But associating with the dough-ball-duel was not high on Phoebe's list of accomplishments she hoped to expound to a future mother-in-law.

People climbed back into their carriages or made their way across the green lawns of Hyde Park, everyone chatting and laughing about the duel they had witnessed. Doubtless, accounts would appear in every newspaper about the event, all of it mocking both the participants and those who had lingered to watch.

Phoebe narrowed her eyes, sweeping the carriages lined up in front of theirs, looking for a particular gentleman in a plum-colored coat. Mr. Richard Milbourne, heir to an estate estimated to be worth eight thousand pounds per annum. Rumor had it he wished to marry before the end of the Season.

From what Phoebe knew about him, he might prove an excellent husband.

"Mr. Fenwick," Caroline called, startling Phoebe out of

her search. Surely, Caroline did not mean to call over one of those men, in public, no less. Mr. Fenwick, coat in place, trotted over to the carriage from his place on the green, wearing a wide grin. He scrubbed his hand through his hair, leaving it a brown mass of waves with blotches of white dough sticking this way and that. His eyes were on Caroline until he was but a few feet from the carriage, and then his gaze flicked to meet Phoebe's glare.

The grin faded abruptly, and his cheeks reddened. Good. Perhaps her sophisticated disapproval put him in mind of where he was and with whom he was speaking.

"Mrs. Kimball," he said, bowing from his place at the side of the path. "Good afternoon."

Caroline laughed, the cheerful sound causing Phoebe to grit her teeth. Everyone in the vicinity would stare at them. "Please, Griffin, we have known each other since our infancy. Call me Caroline."

That brought Phoebe's attention back to her sister-in-law. "I did not know you were so familiarly acquainted with this man." She spoke without thought, then pressed her lips tightly together. But really, she had been shocked into the exclamation.

Caroline was not at all put out. "Of course. Why would I not be? My family and the Fenwicks have been intimately connected for years. Our fathers' estates adjoin one another." Caroline batted her pretty, blonde lashes at Phoebe, but that placating trick only worked on Phoebe's older brother. "Please, allow me to introduce you. Phoebe, this is Mr. Griffin Fenwick. Griffin, this is my sister-in-law, Miss Phoebe Kimball."

Phoebe's good manners forced her to turn to the gentleman, staring down into his twinkling blue-gray eyes as he bowed. He kept his gaze directed at her through the gesture, which made her blink. Men normally did not appraise her so openly.

"Miss Kimball, it is a pleasure to meet you at last. Your sister-in-law spoke of you a great deal last time she visited Essex." He straightened after she gave him a brief nod, his expression still one of amusement.

"I have heard her speak of you, on occasion. My brother had the most to say after meeting you." Phoebe refrained from mentioning that her elder brother, Caroline's husband, mostly commented on the man's ability to make others laugh. Not much else was said about him, in his favor or otherwise. Likely, the man was little more than a fool.

Usually, when someone stared down their nose at Griffin, he did not care. The opinions of others, even pretty young misses with pert noses, were of little importance to him. On more than one occasion he had seen the bores of Society grimace at his antics. But it was rare someone so young refused to see the humor in his escapades, and it gave him pause.

"I rather liked your brother," he told Miss Phoebe Kimball. "A good chap, really." It somewhat surprised him that a man who seemed as eager to laugh as Mr. Joseph Kimball would have a sister with such a stern and disapproving countenance.

The young woman's smile appeared, though it was tight as a miser's fist. Shame. She was likely more than pretty when she smiled. Her eyes slid away from him, back to the line of open carriages finally beginning to stir on Rotten Row.

"Caroline," she said, her delicate eyebrows drawing together in a frown. "Look. Mr. Milbourne is coming closer." She adjusted her posture and widened her eyes.

Griffin raised his eyebrows at Caroline. She met his gaze and shrugged, one corner of her mouth tightening as though to say to him, *I haven't any idea what she sees in him.*

"Have you a wish to meet Mr. Milbourne?" Griffin asked, keeping his tone light. He and Milbourne had gone to Oxford at the same time, and they now belonged to the same club. Griffin rather pitied any woman who wound up with the man. He had no thought for the feelings of others, living only for his own pleasure. Rumor was he had become quite the gambler of late, too, to the distress of his family.

Miss Kimball cut him a look from the corner of her eye. "Do you know him, Mr. Fenwick?"

"Somewhat." Was it his place to tell the young woman the man she wished to meet was a crass and arrogant imbecile? Likely not. He shrugged. "I can introduce you, if you wish."

Noticing more sticky dough upon his shoulder, Griffin grimaced. He must still have quite a bit in his hair. He started combing his fingers through it again, drawing out sticky white clumps into his fingers. The young woman leaned away, though it would be quite impossible for any of the dough to land upon her as she was above and several feet away from him.

"That would make this outing worthwhile for Phoebe," Caroline said, releasing a sigh as she began to fan herself. "Though I am content to have merely witnessed your duel. It was such fun, Griffin."

He grinned at her. "The viscount is an excellent

bowler, I should say. He certainly trounced me, which is all the more insulting since I came up with the idea."

Miss Kimball made a noise of impatience in the back of her throat. "Mr. Milbourne is nearly here," she whispered. "Please, Mr. Fenwick, if you would—?"

"Of course." He opened the door to the phaeton, jumping in to sit across from the ladies. Miss Kimball drew back in surprise, her jaw dropping open, while Caroline covered a smirk with her fan. "You did not expect me to stand in the road to make such an introduction, did you?" he asked, keeping his tone innocent.

Color rose in her cheeks, and the young woman did not appear to know what to say. He winked at her, then turned to the approaching yellow phaeton. "Ah, Milbourne. Good afternoon." The other man was wearing a very purple coat, and a silver waistcoat that looked as though it would not cover his growing middle much longer.

Milbourne, driving himself, slowed his single horse. "Is that you, Fenwick? Do not tell me you caused all the fuss on the green."

Griffin laughed. "Very well, I will not tell you such a thing. Instead, I will introduce you to these fine ladies. Mrs. Joseph Kimball and her sister-in-law, Miss Kimball. Mrs. Kimball and I grew up as neighbors. Ladies, Mr. Milbourne and I attended Oxford at the same time."

Milbourne's eyebrows rose, and he leaned somewhat closer. "Miss Phoebe Kimball? I have heard all about you, of course, but I did not expect to be so fortunate as to receive an introduction." His eyes narrowed almost imperceptibly, as they likely would at an especially good hand of cards.

It was rather unlikely they would run in the same

circles, Griffin supposed, given that Milbourne preferred gaming tables to the marriage mart.

Miss Kimball smiled, though it was something of a subdued expression, and tipped her head to one side. "Oh, it is I who am fortunate to meet you, sir."

Griffin lost interest in their exchange, looking back over the park. He had left his horse tied up beneath trees on the opposite side of the green, and he could see the beast still there, nibbling at the grass. He had nearly decided to excuse himself when he heard Mr. Milbourne ask to call on the young woman.

That brought his attention back to the conversation, and to a blushing Phoebe Kimball. She appeared rather pleased with herself as she gave the man permission to visit and take tea with her the next afternoon.

Caroline was still waving her fan and seemed even less invested in the conversation than Griffin. Given that she was likely Miss Kimball's chaperone, that did not bode well.

"I look forward to coming to know you better, Mr. Milbourne," the unmarried miss said with a simpering smile that looked not at all natural upon her face. He had thought she had rather intelligent brown eyes, but if she sought the company of one such as Milbourne...

"Capitol. Good to see you again, Fenwick. Mrs. Kimball. Miss Kimball." Milbourne tipped his hat to them and went on, grinning rather like a wolf who had been invited into the sheep pen.

Frowning, Griffin looked to Caroline. "You are not really going to allow an association with Milbourne, are you?"

That brought both women's attention to him. "I do not see why not. I know nothing to concern me about the gentleman." Caroline smiled, though the expression appeared tired or strained. She did not seem herself, really. When he looked to Miss Kimball, her eyes were narrowed.

"I do not expect you to understand someone of Mr. Milbourne's reputation," the young woman said, somewhat defensively. "His family is known quite well in London, and I have never heard anyone speak ill of him."

Most likely because speaking of his sort would not be considered polite conversation, Griffin thought. It was not his place to become involved. Surely, Miss Kimball's brother would learn of the meeting and caution his sister. Unless Mr. Kimball knew nothing about Milbourne, either. It was not as though he paid much attention to Society, now that he had procured a wife for himself. He had said as much to Griffin the previous summer.

Griffin shrugged away the troubling thought. "It is none of my business, of course, Miss Kimball. I am certain we all ought to form our own opinions of those we associate with." He tried one of his more charming grins in an attempt to coax her back to good humor. Instead, she wrinkled her nose at him and turned away, as though interested in something on the other side of the road.

Petulant little thing, for all she had a lovely profile.

But it was none of his affair. Griffin smiled at Caroline, wishing her well, then took his leave of them both and descended from the phaeton. He strolled across the green, grinning a bit to himself when he stepped over a particularly large clump of bread dough.

He had brought laughter to more people than he had planned that afternoon. It did everyone a bit of good, he knew, to have something cheerful to speak of rather than the usual gossip or news of the Continental war. With a bit of a sigh, he mounted his horse and went home. His parents would most likely wish for an account of his afternoon before they prepared for dinner and their usual evening entertainment.

Even as he tried to decide which parts of the dough-duel to exaggerate to see his mother laugh, he could not help but think of Milbourne's pleasure at meeting Miss Kimball. It was enough of a distraction to him that when he arrived home, he stopped to speak to the butler.

After all, no one in London knew more about the gossip of gentry and nobility both than the household servants.

"Miss Kimball, sir?" Bastion asked. "Yes, sir. The rumor is she is on the lookout for a husband with a nest as well-feathered as her own. I could not say why, of course. But I do believe this is her third season."

"When you say well-feathered nest," Griffin said, raising his eyebrows, "do you mean that she is wealthy? I did not think Caroline Wynncroft married into a wealthy family."

"Not precisely wealthy, sir." Bastion's forehead puckered as he thought. "But I believe there was some scandal last year, when a man in search of a fortune attempted to court her. He was exposed, of course. Miss Kimball left London, likely in some embarrassment."

That made Griffin nod slowly as he worked out the rest himself. "She would not wish to fall prey to a fortune hunter again, therefore she would look for someone not necessarily in need of her dowry. I suppose that makes sense." He winced, thinking again of Milbourne's rather unsavory habits. Even if the man had money enough at the moment, he might not hold on to it if he continued gambling. And keeping a mistress.

Not that it was his business. Perhaps he could pen a letter to Joseph Kimball and express his concerns. That seemed like the best course of action in such circumstances. Or pay a call on the man. Yes, that would have to do.

Griffin went in search of his mother, his grin more confident now that he had decided upon a course of action.

CHAPTER 2

A LITTLE LUCK

M r. Joseph Kimball had left Town to see to a matter on his father's estate. That was what the Kimball butler told Griffin the next morning when he asked to be admitted into the house. Griffin stared at the butler with confusion.

"What of the senior Mr. Kimball?" Surely, Miss Kimball's father would serve just as well. He need only deliver a warning. It mattered little to whom, so long as the individual cared about Miss Kimball's happiness.

"He did not come to Town this Season," the butler said, somehow looking and sounding stiffer than before.

Griffin took a card from his coat and gave it to the servant. "Here is my card. Will you take it up to Mrs. Joseph Kimball? She and I are friends."

The butler took the card, then placed it on a silver platter on a table near the door. "I am afraid she is resting and is not to be disturbed, sir."

There were very few hours left before Miss Kimball was to entertain Mr. Milbourne. While nothing dire was likely to occur during their casual appointment, it would be best if she were warned not to schedule another. He should put her on her guard, at the least.

Leaving the house with a quick step, Griffin went directly to the rooms he kept in town. When his parents came to London, he usually stayed with them, but keeping his own set of rooms had proven quite handy on more than one occasion. Independence from one's parents assured more felicity and understanding when he made decisions for himself without first consulting them. They loved him, of course, but Griffin needed a place all his own.

He let himself into his rented rooms inside what had once been a very elegant townhouse. Three rooms with doors opening into each other belonged to him. He used one for dining, one as a bedroom, and the largest as a place to entertain guests and relax.

He went into his bedroom where a writing desk sat beneath a wide window. Griffin dropped into the chair and rummaged about in the drawers until he found everything necessary to write a letter.

The moment he dipped his pen in the ink, however, he realized his mistake.

He had planned to write Caroline, but she might not see his letter if she had taken ill. The butler had seemed more than adamant about her remaining undisturbed, after all. No one else was in the house, except Miss Phoebe Kimball herself. Writing a young woman, without parental permission, was most improper.

Griffin tossed the pen down and leaned back in his chair.

Impropriety had rarely stopped him before, but he had never mixed anyone in with his plans without their permission. Miss Kimball would likely object to him taking such a liberty as writing her a personal note.

But then, if she did not know where the note came from, or who had penned it, she would have no reason to be upset.

Thus justified, Griffin took the pen up once more.

Two letters waited for Phoebe in her room, after she had spent a marvelous quarter of an hour in Mr. Milbourne's company.

Perhaps *marvelous* overstated the time spent with the gentleman, but Phoebe needed to be positive. His fortune was similar in size to hers, which meant they would enter into any match made as equals. That was a high mark in his favor.

She took her letters from Lawler, thanking the butler, and went into the study to open them. She recognized the hand on the first, and the thickness of the paper made it clear there was more to the packet than merely a letter.

But it could not be. She had no need of the bracelet, or of the good luck the girls had come to associate with it. Everything in her life went according to plan, no luck necessary.

Yet when she lifted the seal and unfolded the paper, a handkerchief fell to the desk with a light clatter. Phoebe hesitated, then lifted the thin cloth to reveal a bracelet of red round beads. It was from Lavinia. She said nothing extraordinary, but the paragraph explaining the bracelet was of interest.

I know this is a trying time for you, dearest. Please consider wearing our bracelet. I think it will bring you luck—and possibly love—on your husband hunt.

After reading through the letter twice, Phoebe sighed and looked down at the bracelet. There would be no harm in wearing it, even if she did not need any extra good fortune. She could look on the bracelet as a simple trinket, reminding her of her friends and simpler times.

In a moment, she had it wrapped about her wrist. The clasp was one the girls had made certain each of them could easily do up alone. A small *snick* secured the red beads to her wrist, and almost immediately Phoebe felt as though each of her friends stood before her.

Daphne, Marah, Lavinia, and Isabel. How she missed them. They had been as close as sisters during their time at school. But it had been years since they had met up, all together.

With a gentle sigh and a tender heart, Phoebe opened the second letter.

Miss P.K.,

I take no delight in this, but feel you must be warned. Mr. Milbourne is not a man to be trusted. He is swiftly gambling away the family fortune, and will lose yours if you two become connected. There is more which makes him an unsuitable choice for a gentlewoman of good family. Please be cautious in your acquaintance with him.

-A Friend

Phoebe stared at the letter, her heart racing. She read it again, trying to ascertain if she had ever seen the hand-writing before. It was bold, with a slant that felt decidedly masculine. The paper was plain, without any embellishment to suggest a personal stationery. She turned it over and inspected the red-wax seal. A rampant lion.

Her bracelet, the same color as the seal, caught her eye.

No. That was silly. The letters had arrived at the same time, and had nothing to do with one another. The bracelet was just a bracelet. A nervous laugh escaped Phoebe and bounced about the corners of the room.

The note, though. That could be serious.

Phoebe left the study and went in search of the butler. She found him in the entryway.

"Lawler," she said, holding out the letter. "Do you know where this letter came from? It has not been franked, nor does it appear to have come through the post." The lines were too crisp, the paper unwrinkled.

"That letter?" Lawler looked at the seal. "Oh, yes. The little girl who sells flowers near the park brought it to the house. She has brought notes from the Barret-Rye family before, I believe."

Phoebe nodded. The Barret-Ryes were friends of Caroline's who lived on the far side of the park. Caroline had mentioned on a walk one afternoon when they'd passed the girl that they frequently bought flowers from her and sent her on the occasional errand for a few pennies.

"I see. Yes, I think you are correct about the flower girl." But his assumption that the note was from the Barret-Ryes was most certainly incorrect. Surely other families might employ the child in a similar manner. "Thank you, Lawler." Phoebe walked to the stairs, holding the note against her chest.

The words it contained might be a lie. Or she might be

at risk of being misled by a man. *Again*. What had Caroline said yesterday?

April is the month of fools.

"I will not be taken in again," Phoebe whispered. She hurried to her room to fetch her spencer and bonnet. If she made a few calls, she could find the truth for herself.

Griffin walked down St. James's, grinning to himself. He had left his club where several of his friends had recounted his dough-ball duel back to him, laughing all the while. They were placing bets as to what sort of foolish thing he might do next. Some thought he would release an animal from the menagerie, or perform on stage at the Royal Theatre. The betting book had appeared, amid much ribbing, and Griffin quite enjoyed the attention, as anyone would.

He intended to walk a distance before finding a hack to take him home for the evening; any number of black carriages waited on gentlemen who had not brought their own vehicles that evening, but the closest conveyance was not the one Griffin sought. He peered into a few as he walked, looking for signs of age. He preferred to give his funds to those most in need, not the few who had managed to claim the choicest positions near the front doors of gentlemen's clubs.

The flash of a pale face inside one vehicle gave him pause. He took a few steps backward and looked again, certain he was mistaken.

A woman waited in the hack. He looked up at the driver, who purposefully ignored him, then approached. Poor thing had likely come looking for a relative and did not know how to go about getting them out of the club without causing a scene. Women were not allowed, of course, and usually sent servants to deliver important messages to husbands.

Griffin knocked on the window, purposefully looking away. "Madam, if you will tell me who you are waiting for, I will happily fetch the man for you."

There was a yelp from inside, then the window dropped open with a bang, startling him into looking up. Directly into Miss Kimball's face.

"What are *you* doing here?" she asked, her dark eyebrows raising comically high.

"What am I doing here? My club is here. What are *you* doing here?" Griffin stared at her, then looked deeper into the shadows. "Do you at least have a maid with you?"

She gasped. "That is none of your concern."

She was alone. Griffin shook his head. "What are you doing out here, Miss Kimball? Your reputation—"

The door opened, and she reached out to grab the lapel of his coat, stunning Griffin enough that he complied when she pulled him into the coach. He realized what he had done when she shut the door behind him.

"See here, Miss Kimball, I will not be forced into a compromising position with you."

A bark of a laugh followed her momentary silence. "Me? Compromise you? Why ever would I do such a thing?"

That ruffled his pride a bit, but Griffin shrugged. "Who knows? Women are mysterious creatures. For instance, I have absolutely no idea why you would pull me into a dark carriage if you did not have nefarious purposes."

She leaned forward in her seat, allowing the lamplight from outside to illuminate her face. "Nefarious?" She smiled enough to make him almost like her. "I suppose I am behaving rather unusually, but I assure you, my being here has nothing to do with you. I merely had no wish for you to stand there and give me away. I am here for a very specific purpose."

"What might that be, that it requires sitting all alone on St. James?" Griffin adjusted his posture first, his hat second, and then smoothed the lapels of his coat. "Caroline would have a fit, I am certain. She cannot know that you are here."

"No one knows I am here," she stated coolly, looking out the window again. "And I will thank you to tell no one about it. You may leave now, if you wish. No one is upon the street at present."

"What is it you are waiting for? Or whom are you waiting for? Perhaps I can help." That would be the gentlemanly thing to do, of course. The satisfaction of his curiosity was an additional benefit. After the way Miss Kimball had treated him the day before, he had thought her entirely too bent upon propriety to be the adventurous sort.

For several seconds, she bit her bottom lip and stared out the window. Her eyebrows were drawn down, her eyes narrowed as she seemed to think. She looked at him from the corner of her eye, then sighed. "I suppose the fact that Caroline knows you so well ought to count in your favor. Very well. I am waiting on Mr. Milbourne. You may remember introducing us yesterday."

"I do, yes." He looked out the window, a feeling of dread pooling in his stomach. "Are you meeting him here?"

"Heavens, no." She appeared genuinely startled. "I intend to spy on him."

His jaw nearly dropped to the floor. "Spy on him?" He sat back in the seat and took her in with entirely new eyes. He had thought her prim and proper. Arrogant or conceited. But here she played at espionage. "I have seriously misjudged you, Miss Kimball."

She narrowed her eyes at him. "I am not surprised." Whatever she meant by that statement, he could not say.

"At least I can be of some service to you," he said at last, the world trying to right itself in his mind. "Mr. Milbourne will not come out for a few hours yet. He is playing cards."

Her shoulders sunk. "Hours? It is midnight now."

Griffin nodded slowly. She was acting on the information in his anonymous letter. While he had not expected such a dramatic reaction, Griffin's relief she had taken him seriously made him relax. "The game is easily worth a few hundred pounds at the moment. He will play until it is over, then he will play again, whether he wins or loses."

"Does everyone know about his gambling habits?" she asked quietly, notes of anxiety in each word.

"Everyone who pays attention to such things." He shrugged, wincing on her behalf. What would it feel like to be the last one to hear such a thing? At least she had made no commitment to the gambler.

"Gambling is a popular pastime among gentlemen, though," Miss Kimball said quietly.

Griffin shrugged again. "That is not the least of his vices, I am afraid."

She groaned and dropped her face in her hands. "Duped. Again." Without raising from her slumped position, Miss Kimball spoke through her fingers. "Thank you for your time and insight, Mr. Fenwick. You may go."

Could he, when she was obviously in distress? "Miss Kimball, I could see you home if you like—"

Miss Kimball sat up abruptly, her spine straight as a needle and her tone just as sharp. "That is unnecessary." She opened the door to the hackney. "Thank you for your concern. Good evening."

Her swift dismissal, made with a cold tone and her nose in the air, gave him pause. Yet he tipped his head to her, stepped out of the coach, and shut the door behind him. Some people did not know how to show gratitude. Not that he needed effusive praise, but something more than being turned out onto the street as though he had been the one performing a questionable act did not sit well with him. It nearly brought his temper to the surface.

Irritating, unreasonable woman. As much as he had admired the gumption it took to spy upon someone, and the bravery besides, he would not allow himself to like Miss Kimball. He had done her a good turn, nothing more. Griffin was determined to think no more of her, even as he walked into the darkness of the street and heard her hackney pull away.

CHAPTER 3

A SPARRING MATCH

To My Friend,

You have saved me from great humiliation and subsequent despair. I thank you, with all my heart. You cannot know what it means to me to receive your warning at such a time when no one else could advise me. I have made certain Mr. M. will have no reason to believe himself welcome in the future.

Truly, I cannot express the depth of my gratitude. May God bless you.

Sincerely Yours,

P.K.

Griffin arrived at the house of Mr. and Mrs. Carew, and their three sons, barely in time for dinner. He'd been abominably late to all of his appointments that day, ever since he had received the note from Phoebe Kimball. He'd read and reread her words, studied the swirls of her handwriting, and tried to discern how the young woman who had pushed him out of a hack could possibly be the same one who wrote such warm words with an elegant and gentle hand.

The woman was more than the stuffy socialite he had first thought her.

He paused in the foyer of the grand house on Brook Street, making certain his cravat remained presentable. With a quick grin at his own reflection, Griffin followed a footman to the upstairs parlor. The doors opened and Griffin strolled in, ready to find entertainment or make his own.

His eyes landed almost immediately on a woman dressed in pale blue, with flashing gemstones in her hair and a placid expression upon her face.

Miss Kimball.

Fortune had smiled upon him, giving him another opportunity to take her measure. Griffin went immediately to where she stood, listening to Phillip Carew wax eloquent about architecture. Phillip was the second Carew son, the one nearest Griffin in age and a personal friend. The poor fellow had reverted to the topic on which he could speak for hours, long after the eyes of his listeners glazed over.

It could only mean Miss Kimball had done something to make Phillip nervous.

Griffin had better save his friend. "Good evening, Miss Kimball. Phillip."

Dark lashes lowered, Miss Kimball's lips turned down when he addressed them. "Mr. Fenwick. I did not know the Carews were a mutual acquaintance."

"Nor did I." Griffin grinned wider when her frown deepened. Though she appeared to dislike him, he suspected there was a great deal more to her regard for him than that. He would discover it, too. "It is a pleasure to see you again so soon after our last meeting."

Ah, that caused a greater reaction.

The woman's dark eyes widened, momentarily turning fearful.

"A pleasure," she repeated, her eyes cutting to the side as though looking for an escape.

His cheer diminished somewhat. He had not meant to make her afraid, alluding to their meeting the night before. Curse it, this was precisely why his mother had always told him to think before speaking. The lady thought he meant her harm, no doubt.

"Of course, it was also our first meeting, in the park," he said hastily, in an attempt to allay her fears. Her eyes sought his again, and the sharp lines of her shoulders relaxed.

Phillip looked from Miss Kimball to Griffin with an arched eyebrow. "I am pleased you two know one another, even though it is a recent acquaintance." He cleared his throat, looking suddenly over Griffin's shoulder. "Ah, if you will both excuse me. I see someone I must speak to." His awkward exit indicated well enough the excuse had been invented. He bowed and disappeared.

Griffin chuckled, knowing Phillip would thank him later, but when he turned back to Miss Kimball her expression froze him in place.

She had reverted to her cold glare from the park. "Mr. Fenwick," she said, narrowing her eyes and snapping her fan open. "You are making a habit of turning up in odd, and dare I say inconvenient, moments."

Griffin forced a smile. "I am not certain what you mean, Miss Kimball. I thought our last two meetings were rather in your favor, seeing that I provided you a service each time." And tonight, he had also provided a service to Phillip.

Phillip Carew had caused himself a great deal of trouble, of course, entering into a secret engagement with a young woman. But Griffin still assisted him in keeping that secret. It wasn't Phillip's fault the girl had a dragon for an aunt. As soon as her father, a general on the Continent, returned, Phillip would win the general's favor and his daughter's hand.

Until then, Griffin and a few select friends were under orders to help Phillip avoid other young ladies and matchmaking mothers.

Miss Kimball continued to glare at him, brown eyes frostier than New Year's Day.

"Mr. Fenwick, though I am certain you mean well, I cannot agree with you." She moved the fan with enough fervor that the curls above her ear fluttered in the breeze.

Griffin shrugged and tucked his hands behind his back. Perhaps he had misread her letter, somehow. The woman did not have a grateful bone in her body.

"I apologize, Miss Kimball. It was never my intention to cause you distress." He could not simply walk away and leave her alone. Not without being rude.

She nodded her acceptance of his apology, and when their eyes met again, her expression softened somewhat. Then her lips parted as though she might speak—

"Mrs. Carew, dinner is served." The pomposity of the announcement had everyone turning to face the butler who then opened a set of double doors into the dining room.

The line formed, and Griffin found himself escorting the eldest daughter of a wealthy gentleman. As an heir to a most comfortable estate, he ranked a bit higher than other men present. He almost looked over his shoulder to see where Miss Kimball fell into the line, but nudged that bit of curiosity out of his brain.

Griffin took his seat, all smiles for the lovely woman on his right, then he looked to his left and froze. Phillip assisted Miss Kimball into the seat beside Griffin.

Meeting his friend's eyes, Griffin very clearly saw Phillip mouth, *"Help me."*

Drat the man and his covert romance.

Griffin forced his smile brighter. "Miss Kimball. We meet again."

"So it would seem, Mr. Fenwick." Phoebe knew her tight-lipped smile was not precisely polite. Yet who would blame her, given all her disappointments of late?

As a second son, most would not think Phillip Carew a likely match for someone with a modest fortune. But Phoebe had discovered that Phillip stood ready to inherit his maternal grandfather's architectural firm, and eventually the old gentleman's estate. He was also single and had yet to show any interest in a woman during the current Season.

Though she had been thwarted once by Griffin Fenwick's appearance, Phoebe intended to spend the evening getting to know Mr. Carew better.

Phoebe removed her gloves in order to eat, as did the other women at the table. She lifted her spoon and caught the subtle gleam of candlelight on the red beads at her wrist. They did not match her ensemble at all, yet she had slipped them on in a moment of uncertainty. The beads

36

might be unnecessary for good luck, but they were a perfect reminder of her dearest friends.

If only one of those ladies sat next to her, rather than the handsome Mr. Fenwick.

Perhaps she could ignore him and devote her dinner conversation to Mr. Carew.

Griffin Fenwick leaned ever so slightly in her direction. "Miss Kimball, you must tell me how you have enjoyed the Season in London thus far."

Confound it.

"I have been positively delighted and diverted, Mr. Fenwick. There are always so many things to do in Town this time of year." Phoebe took a delicate sip of her soup. Pea soup, with some sort of fowl. It took a great deal of control not to wrinkle her nose.

A new voice, from the other side of the gentleman, spoke up. "You must have quite a list of favorites, given that this is your third Season out."

Heat rushed up Phoebe's neck and into her cheeks, and her gaze darted up to see a girl with gold ringlets lean forward in her chair just enough for the wicked light in her eyes to be seen. Miss Applegate. Daughter of a baronet.

Mr. Fenwick shifted uncomfortably in his seat, his cheerful demeanor faltering for a moment.

Never mind. Phoebe could handle herself. She tried on a smile, the sort one wore to cover a secret. "Indeed, Miss Applegate. I should be happy to give you a list of my recommendations on appropriate entertainments for one so lately come from the schoolroom." It might not be her most subtle barb, but Miss Applegate turned a motley pink before giving her attention to her soup.

Her gaze caught Mr. Fenwick's by chance, but she saw

the twinkle of amusement there, and the way his lips turned upward. He tipped his head, as though in salute.

Phoebe suppressed her smile and gave her soup another cursory sip. "Mr. Fenwick, what are your particular favorite activities? Besides lobbing dough about in London's finer parks."

Rather than appear contrite, or even remotely rebuffed, the man's slight smile grew into an approving grin. "I tend to find amusement wherever I may be, Miss Kimball. Though I do rather enjoy the parks, most of all, and gardens when I can spare the time. Spending time out of doors is far more enjoyable than sitting about in stuffy parlors."

A sentiment she readily agreed with, but she could not let him know that. He was ruining her opportunity with Mr. Carew, after all. "Stuffy parlors? Oh, but all the ladies of London spend our time in parlors, you know. Drinking tea, embroidering, and hoping to entertain callers. What a loss your company must be, when you are out in flower gardens." She turned to the side, sensing Mr. Carew's attention. "As an architect, sir, you must have things to say upon the enjoyment one might find in a well-constructed home."

Mr. Carew's cheeks pinked. He swallowed abruptly. "Well, I am certain—that is to say, my interest lies more in public buildings. But I have set about designing a house. My own, that is. For the future." He stumbled about in his words the way a drunkard might stumble out of a tavern.

Poor man. He must be painfully shy.

Not like Mr. Fenwick, who joined their conversation uninvited. "A future house. If you are to build your own, Phillip, perhaps you should wait until you are ready to wed. I imagine a bride would prefer to have some say in a new construction."

"Oh. Yes. Of course. They are only rough plans, and I should like to consult the future lady of the house." Phillip coughed into his hand, and his eyebrows rose as he looked over her head at Mr. Fenwick, as though he was trying to communicate without speaking.

How odd. And suspicious.

Phoebe turned to Mr. Fenwick, lowering her lashes and curling her lips into a smile. His expression faltered a moment, then returned to cheerful ignorance. Did he mean to pretend she had not caught him frowning darkly at Mr. Carew? Why was Mr. Fenwick determined to put himself into their conversation?

"What of you, Mr. Fenwick? Would you make such concessions for a lady?"

He leaned just a touch over the arm of his chair toward her. "For the future Mrs. Fenwick, of course. But as I have no plans to wed at present, nor any plans to build a new home, I believe I am safe from such a concern." His teeth flashed white as he grinned.

The soup course was taken away, the fish replacing it.

"A true loss for the ladies of London," Phoebe quipped, but her dart had no effect. Mr. Fenwick's eyes crinkled at the corners. "It is rare a bachelor in London would so baldly state that he has no plans to wed, though I imagine a good deal of gentlemen might keep such a desire secret. What, pray tell, causes the hesitation on your part?"

He lifted his cup of wine to his lips, though he kept his gaze upon hers. "It is not hesitation, I assure you. Merely disinterest."

"In marriage or in young ladies?"

"Marriage itself is not an unpleasant idea." He sipped

from his cup at last and lowered it back to the table. "But if I entered into that blessed sacrament with the wrong young lady, I imagine I would equate marriage with torture."

Phoebe wrinkled her nose before hastily recalling a lady ought never to do so in public. "Are your requirements for a bride so particular that you have not come upon one woman who happens to meet them? You must have exacting standards."

"Not at all." His eyes twinkled at her as he twirled his fork in one hand, then speared his fish. "I would prefer a woman of good humor, sound judgment, wit, and the ability to hold a pleasant conversation. That is not asking too much, is it?"

The simplicity of his words could not possibly reveal the entire truth. No man would be content with so little. Her own brother had easily rattled off a list of twenty requirements for the woman he wished to marry. Caroline had fulfilled nearly all of them.

Her next words were something of a dare. "I suppose a large dowry and a pretty face would not matter to you then, Mr. Fenwick?"

Mr. Fenwick finished chewing his bite of food before he made his answer, and Phoebe rather hoped it would prove clever.

"I am fortunate enough that I can marry for love rather than fortune, Miss Kimball. As to 'pretty,' I find that a woman is only as lovely as her character."

Her lips parted, but no retort came to mind. Mr. Fenwick had the audacity to wink at her, then he turned to the woman seated on his right.

Phoebe lifted her fork, the course of the conversation momentarily lost. She had spent more time sparring with

Mr. Fenwick than actually coming to know Mr. Carew. As he apparently believed himself the victor in their verbal sparring, Mr. Fenwick had momentarily ceased blocking her conversation. But he had left Phoebe befuddled. How did she begin anew with Mr. Carew?

The only time Mr. Carew had proved talkative was during his conversation on the history of London buildings. Uninterested though she was, Phoebe seized quickly upon the topic before Mr. Fenwick remembered her.

"Mr. Carew, will you please tell me what you think of the Tower? There is so much history in that old building. How many additions would you say it has had since the time of William the Conqueror?"

Mr. Carew noticeably perked up, and he fairly dove into the topic. "Given that the Tower was built by the Normans, one must start there, and understand where the original foundations existed before London was altered."

As he continued to discuss the type of stone used to build the original walls about the Tower of London, Phoebe looked to the side to see Mr. Fenwick's reaction to her victory.

He actually wore a frown and stabbed at his fish as though the food had done him harm.

Served him right. Everyone knew Mr. Carew's mother wanted all her sons married, which made any one of them fair game. But Phillip Carew's fortune would be in proportion to Phoebe's, making him her favored candidate.

Batting her eyes, Phoebe turned her full attention to Mr. Carew, and tried to understand why he disliked the Tudor additions to London's famous castle so very much.

CHAPTER 4
A TURN ABOUT THE SQUARE

T o My Friend P.K.,

    While I congratulate you on your excellent selection this time, I feel I must offer warning yet again. Mr. P.C. has not yet made it general knowledge, but he is, at present, promised to another. I should hate to see you waste your time—or worse still—your feelings, upon a man who cannot return your sentiments.

    Most Sincerely, With My Good Wishes,

    Your Friend

To My Mysterious Friend,

    I will not bother to speculate how you are so aware of my movements that you know precisely how and when to warn me. We live in London. A thing barely happens before the gossip takes it from one end of the city to the other. I thank you for your warning.

    As I do not know how you come by your information, you will understand that I must verify what you have said before acting upon your advice. Nevertheless, I am most grateful to you.

    Yours, etc.,

    P.K.

Phoebe left the letter to her anonymous friend with the flower girl, then started upon her walk. Berkeley Square was not so fine as Grosvenor Square, but Number Fourteen had been her home during every Season from the time of her childhood. Her father had bought it, nearly new, and she had measured her years by the growing trees in the middle of the square.

A maid walked behind her, just far enough back to give Phoebe the illusion of privacy. This allowed her to pretend, for a brief time, that she was not a maiden in her third London Season, but an independent woman.

Miss Applegate's insinuation two evenings previous, that Phoebe had been unsuccessful in finding a husband the previous years, had nettled her. Unlike most women who went charging about, looking for the wealthiest husband they could attract, Phoebe had first come to London with roses in her cheeks and romance in her heart. She had made that vow to her friends, of course, and had meant it with all the zeal of girlhood.

She had planned everything, perfectly, before stepping foot on London soil. The first half of her Season, she would come to know as many gentlemen as possible, and make new friends who were as good as those she had left behind. There would be one gentleman, she knew, who would stand out. A man worthy of her heart, and the promise she and her friends had made.

Phoebe paused on her walk and looked across the Berkeley grasses to the young trees reaching for the heavens the way she had once reached for her dream of a gentleman to hold her heart.

No such man had ever appeared. No matter. She had

drawn up her plans for her second Season, and just when she thought to give up, she had met Harold Brookston. He had flattered and flirted, made her blush, danced with her at every opportunity. Then he had started pushing for an engagement, and she'd demurred, uncertain of her heart.

That uncertainty had saved her. His family had fled in the night, but they were caught and brought back to London to stand trial. Harold and his father went to debtor's prison, their estate seized by the Crown.

He had wanted her money, and nothing more.

People married for worse reasons. Phoebe knew that.

But she'd fled to the country, humiliated, and shredded her plans to bits. Then she wrote up a new plan, with a list of names. Romance was not for her. She would find another way to happiness in mutual respect. That would be enough.

With such melancholy thoughts distracting her, Phoebe did not notice Mr. Fenwick until he stood at her side. "What are you looking at with such intensity, I wonder?"

She jumped and covered her heart with one hand. "Mr. Fenwick."

He gave her a lop-sided grin and bow. "Miss Kimball. Greetings."

Phoebe glanced toward the trees, then back to him. Where had he come from?

"I must say, Miss Kimball, that running into you is becoming a habit. I cannot yet discern, however, if it is a good one I ought to keep, or a bad one I must attempt to break." He sighed dramatically, then offered her his arm. "What do you think?"

She accepted his escort, almost without thinking about it. "I hardly see that what I think matters. We seem rather doomed to such meetings." She looked down at her bracelet, peeking out at her from beneath the sleeve of her spencer. "Or fated, depending upon your perspective."

Surprise colored his tone. "I had rather expected you to put me in my place again, Miss Kimball. Not offer your agreement upon the matter."

"I have not agreed with you," she argued at once. "And I cannot put you in your place, sir, because I know not where you belong." There. Let him puzzle that out. Odd man.

"I suppose I belong wherever I am at the moment. If we believe in fate, that is." Mr. Fenwick clicked his tongue upon the roof of his mouth. "That would mean, Miss Kimball, that I belong right here. With you."

Phoebe's heart skipped a beat before she saw the glimmer of laughter in his eyes and the upturned corners of his mouth. Of course he had not meant anything serious by such a statement. She hastily put aside her odd reaction to his words.

"Do you ever get tired of teasing?" she asked darkly, shaking her head at him.

"Never. It does little harm, if any, and usually makes people smile." He kept his steps measured, short. Perhaps for her benefit. Perhaps to prolong his time in her company for more verbal torture.

Phoebe's thoughts turned, and an excited sort of flip took place in her stomach. Why not play his game? She could tease and torture as well as he, and it had proved rather amusing at the dinner table the other evening.

That thought gave her the perfect topic to pursue.

"It may surprise you to know, Mr. Fenwick, that I have given some thought to your words from the other evening. On marriage."

He coughed away a small gasp, turning his head from her. His voice sounded strained when he spoke again. "I thought we had said all that was necessary on that particular topic."

"Have we? Or are you merely reluctant to reenter the conversation on the chance that I might come out the victor this time?" She tipped her head to the side and attempted to appear more innocent than conniving.

Mr. Fenwick's eyes narrowed. "I was not aware we were keeping track of points in our conversations, Miss Kimball. But do go on. You have my interest."

"Thank you." Phoebe lowered her gaze to the walk. "I should like to begin the topic, Mr. Fenwick, with an inquiry. I have wondered why a man of your age would persist in claiming no interest in marriage. While I concede that gentlemen may take longer at such a choice than ladies, you are rather in your dotage, are you not?" Teasing him served him right, after he had amused himself at her expense more than once of late.

His head turned abruptly, and she sensed his eyes upon her, studying her. "Dotage, Miss Kimball? I'll have you know I am younger than you are."

Phoebe stopped walking and turned toward him, releasing his arm. "Sir, I cannot believe you would say such a thing. You are not. You must be nearer thirty than twenty." She narrowed her eyes and studied the charming, tiny lines near the corners of his eyes; they grew deeper as he smiled. *At her*. He had a rather nice smile.

"I will have you know that I have only marked my birthday on six occasions." His eyes glittered, bluer than gray in his amusement.

Phoebe crossed her arms over her chest. "That is absurd. Indeed, the most absurd thing I have ever heard."

He mimicked her stance. "I swear to you, on my honor, it is the truth."

Phoebe opened her mouth to argue, then snapped it shut again and stared hard at him. There was a puzzle in his words somewhere, and she would find the answer. Perhaps his family had not done anything on the anniversary of his birth to mark the occasion. That might be what he meant. Yet she had heard, from Caroline, all about the Fenwick family. They sounded as though they were all quite close, and if they had produced someone such as the gentleman before her, they likely did not ignore excuses to celebrate.

"Six birthdays." She wrinkled her nose.

His grin turned almost cocky. He offered his arm again. She accepted it. "Six," he confirmed. "I will wager you have celebrated twenty years of your life passing." Their walk continued, even slower than before.

"I have." Drat and bother. "Six marked birthdays. What happened during the unmarked anniversaries?" She ought to hate how curious he had made her. Yet she had always had a weakness for riddles. Especially those with logical conclusions.

"There were none. Only the six have passed since my birth." He chuckled, sounding far too certain of himself.

Phoebe sighed. "I will think on this, sir."

"Do. Take whatever time you need." He was leading her around the square, she realized. They had passed Number Fourteen several houses before.

"Mr. Fenwick," she said, turning to look up at him. He was taller than she by a head. "Are you very well acquainted with the Carew family?"

His smile momentarily faded, and though he did not look down at her, she sensed caution in the way his eyes narrowed. "Yes. Very well. I consider Phillip to be one of my oldest friends."

"How fortunate for me. I have a question I must ask. A delicate question." She cleared her throat and lowered her eyes to the path upon which they walked. "Is Mr. Phillip Carew already—that is to say, are you aware if he might already have bestowed his affection upon a young lady?"

The gentleman paused, and when she looked up, she saw, for the first time, a very deep line creasing his forehead and a frown upon his face.

"I do not mean to pry," she said hastily. "Or ask you to betray any confidences. I need not know her name. Only if she exists. You see, I had thought to come to know the gentleman better, but if friendship is all that is possible, I should like to know."

He glanced away from her, presenting a profile of a long, elegant nose and strong jaw. He took in a deep breath which expanded his chest, then released it with his answer. "Yes. There is someone Mr. Carew has set his hopes upon."

A flicker of disappointment made her shoulders sag. Her mysterious correspondent had told the truth. She ought to write her thanks again, except she already had, in a way, even before confirming his news.

"Thank you," she said quietly. The day had grown dimmer, and she drew a line through Mr. Carew's name upon the list in her mind. "Would you be so kind as to walk me home, Mr. Fenwick?" She gestured behind them.

"Of course." He turned and offered the opposite arm for her to take. The maid who had been trailing behind them squeaked and hurried to step aside so they might pass her.

Mr. Fenwick was quiet for some time, all the way up

until he assisted her across the street. Delivering her to the very door of Number Fourteen, he released her arm and bowed. "Thank you for your company, Miss Kimball. I enjoyed it."

Though distracted by the rearrangement of her plans, Phoebe curtsied and said what was proper. "It was pleasant to spend a few moments with you, Mr. Fenwick."

The butler opened the door. The maid had already disappeared through the servants' entrance below street level. Phoebe stepped inside, but the instant before the door shut, she had a bolt of understanding.

Phoebe threw the door open again and went to the top of the steps. Mr. Fenwick had already attained the pavement.

"Mr. Fenwick," she called.

He spun, looking up at her. He took a step closer. "Is something the matter, Miss Kimball?"

When her grin burst across her face, her elation taking hold of her, he froze as though stunned. Good. A man like him ought to be surprised once in a while. Phoebe delighted in his full attention as she solved his riddle.

"You were born on a leap day. Then you would be near thirty, but with only six birthdays celebrated."

His grin flashed, and he bowed to her, right there upon the street. Phoebe laughed, then covered her mouth with one hand. What would the neighbors think?

"Good day to you, sir." She spun on her heel, walked into the house, and did not look back as the befuddled Lawler shut the door behind her.

CHAPTER 5
LIST OF SUITORS

To My Unknown Friend,

I have confirmed what you told me, sir. I must thank you again, even as I cross Mr. Carew's name from my list. That must sound callous to you, that I keep a list of potential suitors. Or perhaps you understand. I am inclined to think you a sympathetic man, given your kindness to me thus far. You must know something of what it is like for ladies, to risk our future happiness upon men we hardly know by more than reputation.

It occurs to me that I might save myself time, having a friend such as you, by sharing my list. If this is presumptuous, do forgive me. But this may save you from future correspondence with someone as woefully uneducated on the bachelors of London as I seem to be.

What think you of these gentlemen? I have listed them alphabetically by surname.

Mr. Henry Brockton

Sir William Carter

Mr. Bartholomew Kenley

Mr. Howard Lambleigh

Lord George Pewton

Mr. Alfred Waymont
Yours Most Gratefully,
P.K.

To The Clever P.K.,

While some might find your list-making presumptuous, I am only intrigued. You appear to be an intelligent woman. You have given your future a great deal of thought, and I am most sympathetic toward you. Here is your list given back, with my notations.

Mr. Henry Brockton (A slave to his mother. I cannot imagine an independent woman enjoying such a thing.)

Sir William Carter (Has announced his intentions to marry a Frenchwoman of his acquaintance.)

Mr. Bartholomew Kenley (A possible candidate, if one does not mind his obsession with insects.)

Mr. Howard Lambleigh (He is a confirmed bachelor with no interest in the fairer sex. Not even a lady as lovely as you.)

Lord George Pewton (While an agreeable man, I must warn you: his hair is not his own.)

Mr. Alfred Waymont (I cannot imagine you wishing to spend more than a moment in conversation with him. He is intolerably stupid.)

My friend, I cannot say what it is you see in these gentlemen. There is no pattern I can detect here, or else I might provide you with a list of men who are more suitable candidates. Do share your requirements with me, P.K., and I will do my best to aid you in your search.

Most Humbly,
Your Friend

Griffin waited in the park, having an idea when Miss Kimball would appear to collect his letter from the flower girl, Anna. The child had agreed to keep his identity a secret, and keep acting as messenger, without even asking a copper of him. She seemed delighted to take part in an intrigue, and he promised to purchase flowers from her every day for the rest of the Season.

He checked his watch, then glanced up at the gray sky. If it rained, Miss Kimball might change her plans. He would need to change his, too, given that he had no umbrella with him.

At three o'clock she appeared, wearing a walking dress and bonnet festooned in emerald green ribbons. She had no maid, which meant she did not mean to go farther than the square. Perhaps she would only pick up her letter and then vanish again inside the house.

As soon as she was on the walk, her back to where Griffin stood in the shade of a tree, he started to follow. Not because he wished to speak to her, necessarily. But seeing her reaction to his letter would amuse him. Finding fault in each of her listed bachelors had proved far too easy.

Not that he had wanted her to cast them all aside. But he had instinctively known not a single of the six men were worthy of a match with someone as bold and intelligent as Miss Kimball. It would take a different sort of man to make her happy, of that he felt certain.

Miss Kimball retrieved her letter from the flower girl and kept walking, perhaps to complete a circuit around the square. She opened the letter and read as she walked, while he kept pace several yards behind her. He was close enough to hear her giggle. The light laugh, at something he had written, gave him reason enough to smile with satisfaction.

Griffin did not hail her until he saw her put the paper in her reticule. Then he called out, "Miss Kimball, is that you?"

She stiffened and looked over her shoulder at him. "Mr. Fenwick." She stopped walking, and he quickened his step until he reached her side.

"We meet yet again."

"So we do." She folded her hands in front of her, the reticule bearing his letter dangling from her wrist. "What brings you out to Berkeley Square today?" She glanced up at the gray clouds. "In such uncertain weather."

"A desire for a walk. I found the park here to my liking, when last we met." He motioned to the trees and well-kept grasses. "Though it is horribly named."

"I do not suppose Berkeley Rectangle would sound as lovely, or as though it might rival Mayfair and Grosvenor Squares." Miss Kimball's lips twitched, though she did not fully smile. "Mr. Fenwick, I was correct when I settled upon your birthdate at our last meeting, wasn't I?"

Griffin bowed, theatrically. "You were most correct. I was born on February the twenty-ninth, in 1784."

Her eyes brightened, and she leaned slightly closer, though a foot of space still separated them. "So you have been alive eight and twenty years, with only six birthdays, because the year 1800 had no Leap Day. Am I correct?"

He grinned at her. "You are."

"You must take great delight in vexing people with that riddle." She did not laugh, though he suspected she wished to do so. "That brings me all the way back to my original question, sir. A man of your advanced *years* seems oddly opposed to the idea of matrimony. Why is that?"

Griffin shrugged. "As I have said, I have not found a lady to my tastes."

"Pity for you." An ominous rumble rolled across the sky, causing Miss Kimball to look up and assess the clouds. "Dear me. It seems neither of us will have our walk."

"Afraid of a little rain, Miss Kimball?" he asked, disappointed she would leave before they'd had a chance to enjoy a verbal duel.

"I am afraid of ruining my bonnet." She touched one of the swirling green ribbons.

"Then I will walk you to your door." Griffin glanced at the reticule on her wrist as she put her hand upon his arm. "Are you not particular about your choice of gentleman, Miss Kimball? I imagine you are on the hunt for a husband, as every single woman in London is on the hunt."

"You make it sound as though I actually have a wide variety of choices." She shook her head, her eyes upon her house rather than on him or the park. "No woman truly does, you know. I am limited by my family's position in Society—"

Griffin interrupted. "Which is fair, given your address." Berkeley rivaled Grosvenor when it came to fashion.

Her eyes narrowed. "My father was fortunate to purchase the house at a time when it was quite affordable. But as I said, my family is not noble; my father is only a gentleman. That narrows the options. Then there is the matter of my dowry; it is too small to tempt those looking to increase their riches or save themselves, yet my family connections are not remarkable enough to entice those that are solvent and only looking to better position themselves in society. We also must take into account my age and appearance. The pool of gentlemen narrows still more with other factors, such as my determination to have intelligent conversation rather than simper at a man as most would desire."

Griffin laughed, a hearty sound that made her shrink and look about as though to make sure he had not drawn attention to them. They crossed the street to her house, but Griffin did not give up her arm immediately.

"Any man who would censure you for speaking your mind would only do himself a disservice." Griffin looked down at her, wondering if he dared try for an invitation into her home. It would save him from the rain and provide entertainment.

What made him laugh turned her sober. "It intrigues me that you think so. My own brother is forever telling me to curb my tongue."

"That is a shame. I find myself amused whenever we have an opportunity to converse."

"Amused?" she asked, eyebrows drawing downward.

Griffin nodded and released her arm. "It is rare a woman speaks her mind as you do."

"And a woman speaking her mind is...amusing." Her tone remained flat, which he ought to have taken as a warning.

Griffin only widened his smile as he continued speaking, ready to explain how much he enjoyed their verbal battles. "Of course. It is refreshing to hear a woman converse with such lightness and wit. Most cannot take what you say seriously—"

Miss Kimball raised her hand, halting him mid-sentence. "That is quite enough." Then she balled that delicate gloved hand into a fist, lowering it to her side while her cheeks turned red. "Most, in fact, do *not* take what I say seriously. I always thought that a mark against *their* intelligence, not my own."

As she spoke, Griffin's horror grew. Something had gone terribly wrong in their conversation. "Miss Kimball, if you will let me explain—"

She cut him off again, at the same moment a large raindrop fell past the brim of his hat. "I have no desire to converse further. I apologize for ending your entertainment this afternoon, but the show cannot go on in the rain. Good day, Mr. Fenwick." She turned from him and ran up the steps. The door opened and when it slammed shut behind her, the sky broke open above.

Griffin stood like an addle-pated dunce, staring at the closed door. The rain did not care that it soaked him and came down all the harder.

At last he turned, walking away. What a fool he was. Even if they had come along in their relationship, apparently, she knew him less than he did her. He needed to mind his tongue. The conversation had turned too quickly, and now he needed to make amends. But when? And more importantly, *how*?

Phoebe paced her bedroom, the glow of the gas lamp the only light. None came from outside, despite the early evening hour, due to the heavy clouds storming above Town. The rain beat against her window, the sound soothing her troubled thoughts.

The letter from her anonymous friend lay open upon her writing desk, a blank sheet of paper beside it.

"Do share your list with me…"

Dare she? Having one man laugh at her that day had

shaken her. Mr. Fenwick had seemed like the sort of man one might befriend, but knowing he only spoke to her because she *amused* him had stung.

Phoebe put her hand over the red beads of her bracelet, rolling the accessory down to her wrist again. How she missed her friends. If only they were near to one another and could laugh away their troubles as they had at school.

What would they advise?

She went to the desk and sat, staring at the neat hand-writing of the man with the rampant lion seal. Who was he, and why had he taken an interest in her? Enough of an interest to warn her not once, but twice?

He had to be a gentleman. At least, that was what she hoped. But was he an elderly fellow merely doing her a kindness? Somehow, she doubted it, given the firm hand he used. And the humor in his words.

It was dangerous for a woman to write to a gentleman, let alone a stranger.

But the little flower girl would warn her if there was something amiss, wouldn't she?

The memory of Griffin Fenwick's smirk, his hurtful words, goaded her at last.

Biting her bottom lip, Phoebe took up the pen.

CHAPTER 6

AN EVENING OF DANCING

M y Dear Friend,
        I am not certain many would call me clever. How
clever is it, for example, to write out one's hopes and wishes to a
complete stranger? I will have to trust to your honor, sir, whoever
you might be.

I suppose I wish for the usual things in a gentleman, in terms of
health and general good nature. But when I think on those things
that I most hope for, that I want to be part of my life, I find myself
hoping for a generosity of spirit. I also wish to find a man who will
be an attentive and kind father, as my father was, yet how can one
know such a thing? I would hope for a gentleman who will view me
as his equal in our marriage.

As you can see, these things are quite impossible to know about
a gentleman. No amount of afternoon carriage rides, ballroom
meetings, or afternoon teas will reveal so much about a person's
character.

But worry not. I do not expect you to find such a companion for
me. For now, if you might point me toward someone of honor and
financial stability, I will be pleased enough. This will be my last
Season in London. I suppose I ought not be too particular.

With all my gratitude,
P.K.

To The Charming P.K.,

Allow me time to ponder on your requirements. I do think they ought to be requirements, as each item is most reasonable and understandable. Why should any woman settle for less than a gentleman with whom she can have happiness as well as mutual respect and devotion?

You mentioned this is your last Season. Might I be so bold as to ask why?

Yours, Etc.,
A Friend

Phoebe bit her lip in an attempt to darken it from a shade of coral to something more like cherries. She stood before a mirror in a withdrawing room at the Countess Vailmoore's annual ball. Then she turned to inspect her hair, pushing a stiff curl back into a pin.

"Phoebe, you look lovely. Do stop fussing." Caroline took Phoebe's hand and gave it a gentle tug. "Your brother is waiting for us in the ballroom, and you *know* how Joseph dislikes balls. We ought not leave him to his own devices too long."

"Of course." Phoebe turned away from the mirror, her stomach twisting. It was no use delaying; she had to go up to the ballroom. Her brother was not the only one who disliked swirling about in a crowded room, filled with the smells of too many perfumes and the noise of a hundred or more people.

But ballrooms were where matches were made. Phoebe needed to meet new gentlemen and construct a new list, with her old list pulled apart by her mysterious friend. As his advice on bachelors had proven correct twice, Phoebe trusted the man knew what he was doing when he gave her warning. Though she did not know exactly how to avoid settling for less than her ideal gentleman. Not if she hoped to be wed that year.

Starting over again when the Season was half over daunted her. Not that anyone would suspect as much, given her poise. Or so she told herself.

Before she entered the ballroom, Phoebe touched the bracelet, this time hidden beneath her long, ivory gloves. Tonight she wore a gown of yellow, trimmed in lace. The cheerful color reminded her of daffodils, her favorite flowers.

Phoebe came to the foot of the staircase where her hand landed upon the rail. She swallowed once, twice, and then looked up to begin her ascent.

Griffin Fenwick stood at the top of the stairs, leaning against the rail on one elbow as he watched her. One corner of his mouth went upward when their gazes connected. He wore a rich brown coat that reminded her of chocolate and a yellow waistcoat that nearly matched her gown. His hair had been tossed about expertly, given it a windblown look that only increased the charm of his appearance.

Not that she would be charmed. Not when she remembered too well the insult he had given her when last they had spoken. He thought her conversation amusing, not to be taken seriously, and for a woman to speak her mind—well. Dwelling upon that would not improve her mood.

Setting her chin at a level a notch or two above where she normally held it, Phoebe took up her gown in one hand then allowed the other to glide along the banister as she walked up. Let him make light of her intelligence if he wished. She would not spend another moment entertaining Mr. Fenwick.

He pushed away from the rail as she approached and bowed when she attained the landing. "Miss Kimball, good evening. I am pleased you could come."

He spoke as though he had issued the invitation rather than the countess.

"Mr. Fenwick," she said, not even bothering to meet his gaze. She stared past him toward the ballroom. "I had no idea you would be present." Though tempted to sweep by without another word, Phoebe had no desire to give anyone the cut direct. There were enough other people standing about in the hall to notice if she behaved that rudely.

"Oh." He sounded disappointed. "Caroline did not tell you?"

Phoebe winced and finally looked at him. "What ought my sister-in-law to have told me?" She knew, when she saw his smile reappear, that he'd had something to do with the invitation that had surprised her when it had arrived.

"The countess is a friend to my mother, and she has met Caroline often enough that when I suggested she extend the invitation to your family, she agreed at once. I am delighted you are here." He did not seem to boast. The cheerfulness in his tone sounded genuine.

How could the man prove both irritating and charming?

Gritting her teeth, Phoebe offered him a tight smile. "Most kind of you to think of us, Mr. Fenwick."

He offered his arm, and she had no choice but to take it. "Might I secure a set of dances with you, Miss Kimball? The next set to begin, if you have not yet promised them elsewhere."

Dreadful man. Unless she wanted to spend the whole of the evening in a chair, she had to agree.

"My first set is yours, Mr. Fenwick." If only he did not appear so pleased, she might have forgiven him. He did not seem to understand, not in the slightest, that she held him in some contempt.

They had barely entered the ballroom, which was actually several large rooms with doors flung open to connect them all, when the music ended. Their first engagement upon the dancefloor was to begin at once.

Phoebe saw Caroline and Joseph standing near the wall. When they spotted her, Caroline's expression changed from merely cheerful to something bordering on excitement. Joseph, ever the protective older brother, merely raised his eyebrows. If Mr. Fenwick noticed them at all, he gave no indication as he swept her toward the couples arranging themselves upon the floor.

The countess never gave out invitations on a whim, as all of Society knew, so her ball could not be called a *crush*. But thirty couples stood ready to dance, and more lined the walls. A set would easily take up half an hour, and perhaps a quarter more depending on the forms. Giving so much time to Mr. Fenwick made Phoebe sigh as she took up her position. Finding enough gentlemen to repopulate her list of eligible bachelors in a single evening had already felt like a challenge without such devotion of time to someone completely unsuitable.

As she stood across from the gentleman, Phoebe kept her expression bored. The man seemingly went through life with the goal of self-amusement. She would give him nothing to laugh over that evening.

He grinned at her anyway.

"I have been pondering something, Miss Kimball." He stepped forward and took her hand, raising it above them both and stepping back again.

"Have you?" Phoebe refused to show interest, pretending to concentrate on the movements of the dance.

"Yes. Your name."

She did not trip, but she did narrow her eyes at him. She lightly skipped to one side as the steps called for. "I cannot see how my name could possibly give you more than a moment's thought."

"Your Christian name is quite lovely and unique. I cannot say I know of many ladies with such a name. It comes from mythology, I believe. Is it not the name of a Titaness? The first ruler of the moon, according to the Greeks." He smiled as though he had said something particularly clever.

Phoebe felt her nose wrinkle before she hastily reminded herself such an expression was not ladylike. "I do know the origins of my name, sir."

"Of course. But I wonder how it came to be chosen for you. Knowing such things, I believe, is telling." He did not appear the least put off by her expression. The dance took them away from each other for several moments. When she returned to stand before him he spoke as though there had been no interruption. "Who named you? Your father or mother?"

Though reluctant to engage in any conversation which might be perceived as meaningful, Phoebe knew he would not allow her to ignore the question entirely. "My mother suggested it. Her Christian name is Mary. She never liked that there were a great many who shared her name."

"She wished your name, and you, to be unique." Mr. Fenwick nodded sagely, though his eyes brightened. "My mother named me with the same thought. Everyone on my father's side argued with her, thinking I ought to be named something sensible like William." His grin flashed as he walked around her and bowed to another lady before returning. "She said, and my father agreed, that she should like me to stand out among gentlemen rather than merely be sensible."

"Given what you were up to the day we met, I should say you succeeded in fulfilling her expectations." Though likely not the way the woman had expected. Despite her earlier commitment to avoid being amused by the man, Phoebe had to smile a touch at that.

He laughed aloud, drawing attention from other dancers, including smiles from several females.

A gentleman with such open good humor was rather rare, especially in a ballroom where every man was either hunted or on the hunt himself. Mr. Fenwick's above average good looks likely contributed to the indulgence of his humor. His bright eyes and dark hair, his lean and tall stature, would pull eyes in his direction even had he frowned.

"Griffin is still more unlikely a choice than a Greek god's name." Phoebe snapped her mouth shut over the observation.

"I know." He took her hand again and moved in close, staying so a second longer than the other gentlemen in the line of the dance. As though he had rather be near her than keep perfect time. For an instant, his grin turned into a soft smile, and an emotion she could not name appeared in his eyes. Whatever it was, it made her heart skip most traitorously.

He stepped away, and she released her breath without knowing when she had begun to hold it.

His merry smile reappeared. "My mother was rather enamored with a Grecian fresco with a griffin standing guard over a fallen man. She and my father brought me up to be a protector, as all gentlemen should be, of those who stand in need."

Phoebe cleared her throat, impressed despite her desire to remain otherwise. "A noble calling, indeed. Do you feel you have honored their wishes?"

"Not perfectly, but I have tried."

Her lips parted, but Phoebe could not think what to say. Most men of her acquaintance would have boasted of such a trait, or protested in a way that reeked of false-humility. She detected neither in the way he spoke. The last strains of the orchestra signaled their time to bow and curtsy to one another.

As she stood, she barely noticed which couples left the row and who arrived. Phoebe's gaze remained on Griffin Fenwick, who spoke to the gentleman on his left with animation. Phoebe recognized the man, but could not put a name to him immediately.

"Your partner dances well, Fenwick," the man said, casting Phoebe a polite smile, though he did not address her directly. They must not have been properly introduced.

Griffin's wide smile was his first answer, before he surprised her with his words. "Indeed, Miss Kimball's grace lends at least some dignity to my own limited abilities." More modesty, for he danced as finely as any man she had ever partnered. "After this dance, if you are very fortunate, the lady will allow me to introduce her properly."

Phoebe lowered her eyes, feeling a blush creep into her cheeks. It was thoughtful of Griffin—she suddenly could not think of him as anything else—not to assume he could make introductions without her approval. His words had been kind.

Why, again, had she been angry with him? It took some thought to remember.

Griffin started to relax at last. Though Phoebe had begun the evening with a cold demeanor, by the time the second dance in their set began she had warmed considerably to him. Her smile appeared more, rendering her already lovely face more beautiful. Here was the girl who had walked with him in the park, before he'd muddled things at her doorstep.

It had taken Griffin time to sort out how his conversation with her that day had turned into a low moment. Arranging for the Countess Vailmoore to invite the Kimballs to her ball had been the first step in his apology, though Phoebe did not yet know it. The next step would be to offer up the words themselves, and the final must be the introduction of several eligible gentlemen to her.

Except Griffin found himself rather wishing he could ask her to dance again. Perhaps reserve another set, or the supper dance at the very least.

"I find myself wondering, Mr. Fenwick, what you do when you are in Town. Do you come for the Society or for another reason entirely?" Phoebe asked, drawing him out of his study of her smile.

"I come for the company. I enjoy being among friends," he admitted. "Though I have an uncle in the House of Commons—my father's younger brother. We support him with our presence, and our connections. He represents our little corner of England to great credit. Where we are, everyone is of the opinion that sheep need more rights." As loathe as Griffin was to discuss politics, he enjoyed the way she laughed at his mention of the sheep.

"Your wooly population must be quite pleased if he represents them well." She did not hide her smile again. "I confess, my favorite part of the Season is rarely the balls. I rather like all the opportunities presented to see new things. I dearly love plays, though I know it is not the fashion to admit to enjoying them."

Griffin sighed deeply. "A sorrowful state of things, to be certain. Merely because no one goes to see the actors and actresses, but to spy upon the other boxes."

Phoebe danced with a lightness he had not seen in her character before. Upon their first meeting, he had thought her too staid. But coming to know her, and getting glimpses of her character still more through her letters, gave him leave to like her a great deal. How could he not, when the only things she most wished for in a husband was a man who would be both a generous husband and kind father? She had not mentioned the wish for a title, for a certain amount of land or wealth, a house in town, or someone excessively athletic or handsome.

His hand grasped her just above the wrist as they

completed a turn, and he felt the presence of a beaded wristlet. Was it the same he had seen before? She had not been without it since he first noticed the red upon her wrist.

They were nearly down the line of couples, which meant their time together would soon end. Given the way other gentlemen had been watching Phoebe as he promenaded her along, he would not get more than a moment or two to escort her from the floor before there was a clamor for introductions.

Which meant it was time for his apology.

Griffin sobered. "Miss Kimball, though this is not ideal timing, I fear I will not have the ability to offer you a sincere apology if I do not make it now."

She blinked at him, and then her expression clouded over. She turned away, walking beneath the joined hands of another couple, then returned to him. "I do not know what you mean, Mr. Fenwick."

"The other day, upon your doorstep, I misspoke. I only wish to tell you that I am sorry for speaking like a bumbling fool. I would never wish to offer you insult. I rather like conversing with you, and I wish to be friends."

Her cheeks turned a becoming shade of pink, and he felt his chest warm in response.

Phoebe took hold of her skirt, preparing to curtsy, and he clenched his fists at his side waiting for her acceptance of his apology. "Mr. Fenwick, of course you are forgiven. Thank you."

Relieved, he offered up his final bow, and then held his hand out to her. Her fingers slipped into his palm, and despite the material of their gloves between them he would have sworn in that moment there was a very real physical connection. His heart leapt, and his grip tightened upon her.

No fewer than four gentlemen converged upon them, as he had known they would, and the moment was lost. Given the brightness of her greeting to each of the men, Griffin doubted he would be granted another opportunity to engage her hand.

The disappointment he felt upon watching her walk away on the arm of another ought to have surprised him.

"Griffin."

He jolted and looked down at Caroline Kimball.

"Oh. Good evening, Caroline." He realized his greeting lacked warmth and smiled rather hastily to make up for it.

She laughed and took his arm. "Do not sound so happy to see me, sir, or my husband may get jealous."

He relaxed, then looked again to where Phoebe smiled at her new partner. "I would not wish to stir such an emotion in one who loves you, Caroline."

"No. I imagine not." Why did she sound so sly as she spoke?

Griffin looked down at her again, but something told him he ought to change the subject quickly. "I hope you are enjoying your evening."

"Very much, thank you." Caroline peered at him most thoughtfully, then turned her attention to her sister-in-law. "Thank you for displaying Phoebe's dancing skills so well, and introducing her to so many. I am afraid I have not been an ideal sponsor this Season."

"I am certain you are doing quite well," he said at once, purposefully guiding her to walk away from the dancers. "Though I had wondered why it is you are here and not the senior Mrs. Kimball."

"Oh, did you not know?" Caroline's expression turned

serious, her eyebrows drawn down along with the corners of her mouth. "Dear me. The family does not mean to keep it a secret, of course, though I suppose we have not discussed it much outside of our own home and friends." She looked to the wall of chairs, where her husband conversed with other married men.

"If you do not think you should tell me," Griffin said, though his curiosity rose, "then please do not. I would not like you to betray any confidences."

Caroline shook her head. "It is not a secret, as I said." Then she sighed. "Last autumn, my mother-in-law was struck rather suddenly. Apoplexy, her doctor said. She has improved a great deal, though she could not even speak for a time. I am afraid she is not able to move about as freely as she once did, and she thought her presence in London would hurt Phoebe's ability to focus on the task at hand."

The task at hand, of course, was to find a husband. Griffin relaxed and looked out to where Phoebe danced, immediately finding her among the throng. His eyes were drawn to her rather like a magnet to metal. "I imagine someone of such a kind nature as Miss Kimball would be more concerned with her mother's well-being than her own."

"That is precisely true of Phoebe." Caroline's smile appeared almost sorrowful. "Last Season, Phoebe kept apologizing for entertaining that scoundrel of a suitor. She takes things very much to heart. My sweet sister-in-law puts burdens upon her shoulders when they are not hers to bear."

Griffin added that to what he knew of Phoebe, unsurprised, and his heart softened toward her still more. He ought to have been alarmed. Yet Griffin had known the moment he saw her that evening, all pretty uncertainty at the foot of the stairs, that his feelings toward the idea of marriage were shifting.

The list of suitors he had begun to compose for her, as her anonymous friend, needed one more name added to it.

His own.

CHAPTER 7
A CALCULATED RISK

To My Friend,

    You are bold, sir, to ask such a personal question. But given that the nature of our correspondence has been most personal, I will answer your inquiry. This will be my last Season in London because I am rather exhausted. Constantly putting myself on display has worn at my confidence, my mind, and my heart. Rather than carry on as some do, I will retire to my family's home. It feels more dignified than putting myself upon the marriage market for a fourth year.

    Perhaps you already know, my dear friend, but I enjoyed myself at the Countess Vailmoore's ball last evening. I met many gentlemen. Have you already learned their names? Are you prepared to tell me which of them is suitable and which I ought to avoid?

    I confess to looking forward to your notes. Though I do not know who you are, I appreciate the kindness you have shown in your words and advice. I wonder if you look forward to my letters at all? Regardless, I hope this note finds you in good health and happiness. I remain

    Your Friend,

    P.K.

.   .   .

Phoebe sat at her desk, reading again what she had written. It was a dangerous game to play, writing a complete stranger. Yet she could not bring herself to tear the note to pieces, to throw it away. And her anonymous friend's letters she kept bundled in her desk, a red ribbon matching the rampant lion seal and her bracelet holding them together in a tidy packet.

If her friends learned of her exchanging letters with an unknown gentleman, what might they say?

Marah would doubtless disapprove. As kind as she was, she was one to follow rules. Usually. Lavinia would worry. She did tend to mother the girls when they were together at school. Isabel's reaction was not one she could be certain of. But Daphne—Daphne *listened*. Daphne was also in Town this Season.

A stab of guilt made Phoebe wince. It was her fault that they had not seen each other more often. Phoebe had kept herself far too busy of late. And their family's social circles did not overlap enough for accidental meetings.

Phoebe determined to write her friend at once. She took out a clean sheet of paper and tapped her pen to her lips as she thought.

To Miss Windham,

My dearest Daphne, I have missed you so.

She wrote a full paragraph on her doings, which parties she had attended and those observations on Society surest to make Daphne smile. Practical she may be, but that only made the impractical things of Society more laughable to her.

She found herself including the dough ball duel for just that reason, and if she described a certain oddly named gentleman with more detail than anyone else, it was only because he had proved so amusing.

Halfway down her paper, Phoebe realized she could not reveal information about her mysterious friend. Not in a letter. Perhaps in person.

Daphne, would you be willing to come for tea later this week? As much as I can tell you in a letter, I can divulge so much more in person. Especially as there is one topic of a most delicate nature I would address, seeking your advice. Do say you will come.

She finished her note with a suggestion for an afternoon three days hence, then signed her name with a flourish. After she sealed the letter, she looked again at the one for her secret friend.

If only she knew his name. But no. It was better not to know. If she knew, she would be far too tempted to seek him out. Instinctively, Phoebe felt they would get along quite well. Especially if he was a bachelor.

To A Charming Lady,

Each time one of your notes is slipped into my hand, I cannot help but be glad. Your observations are intriguing, your wit appreciated. While our communication is certainly unusual, I am grateful I dared send that first note.

I have given more thought to your new list of eligible gentlemen. There are men in London whom I believe capable of such devotion and attentiveness as you would wish in a potential suitor. They are men of honor, from good families where the qualities you seek are present. I hope that by providing you this list you will find the right person to make introductions for you.

Mr. Walter Elton, of London, a Barrister

Mr. Griffin Fenwick, of the Watford Fenwicks

Mr. William Nelson, of Hampshire

Mr. Peter Thackery, of the Kenwick Thakerys

Mr. George Waverton, of Bristol

This list will give you a place to start. These gentlemen are all known to me, and I would trust them to treat any lady with respect and gentility.

Is London to your liking this Season, P.K.? I do hope you have taken time away from your busy schedule to enjoy the art collections, theaters, and other cultural delights. I myself will go to the theater to see a revival of Cumberland's play, The Eccentric Lover. *It is a comedy you may perhaps enjoy, given that it is based upon a courtship which goes horribly awry. It will be the first time the play has been performed at Covent Garden Theater since its rebuilding.*

I wish you good fortune, my dear friend.

Yours, etc.,

A Friend

The risk Griffin took was calculated when he sent that letter. He had, as promised, provided Phoebe with the names of eligible gentlemen. Slipping his own in among them would at least give her pause. If she had not yet considered him a candidate for courtship, her mind might at last bend that way on the word of her anonymous friend.

He gave the letter to the girl selling flowers along with several extra pennies if she would abandon her flowers and deliver the note immediately. She happily tucked the note in her basket of posies and skipped away, leaving Griffin to follow behind. He would wait no more than five minutes after the note was delivered to call upon Phoebe.

He had not called upon her the day before, as the other men she had danced with would have been there during her at-home hours.

Though normally not one to plan out things, Griffin knew winning Phoebe Kimball would require an effort. She would receive the note from her anonymous friend, read his name upon the list, learn of the play, and then Griffin would arrive inviting her to the theater that very same evening. Her mood would already be favorable, if she truly enjoyed writing to him.

When the requisite time had passed, Griffin passed the smiling flower girl, paid her for a posy, then went up to the door and knocked.

He entered the parlor where Phoebe sat, the letter folded in her hand, and his heart began beating at twice its usual rhythm. She tucked the letter behind her back, a blush fading from her cheeks as she curtsied. Today she wore a gown of white, with a teal shawl around her shoulders and the red beaded bracelet again on her wrist. The jewelry must hold some sort of personal meaning for it to be upon her person so often.

"Mr. Fenwick, I was not expecting you."

Griffin chuckled and bowed. "I hope my visit is not as unpleasant as it is unexpected."

Caroline's voice surprised him from where she stood near the window. "How could your company ever be unpleasant, Griffin?" He had not even noticed his friend. Phoebe had taken all his attention at once.

"Caroline, I am glad to see you. Have you recovered from the ball sufficiently?" He darted a quick look at Phoebe when she lifted a book from the couch, tucking the letter inside the cover. He cleared his throat. "I—I recall you were quite tired when you left."

"Yes, thank you for your concern." Caroline's sly smile had returned. She looked from Griffin to her sister-in-law. "Phoebe enjoyed herself immensely. I think she would have gone to another ball the very next evening had I not begged for an evening at home."

That remark gave Griffin permission to turn his attention fully back to the unmarried lady. "It was a fine evening. I do not think I saw you without a partner even once, Miss Kimball."

"Indeed, I was quite fortunate in partners." Phoebe clasped the book in one hand and gestured with the other to a chair. "Will you sit with us, Mr. Fenwick? Perhaps take some tea and cake?"

"I would very much like that." Griffin took the chair, and Phoebe resumed her seat upon the couch. Caroline came and joined her. "I must apologize for not calling right away. I am afraid some family matters arose which required my attention." That was at least in part true. He had entertained his mother when he ought to have been paying his call. "But I do have a peace offering for you ladies, if you will accept my apology."

"Is it an offering then, or a bribe?" Phoebe asked, her eyebrows raising while her rosy lips slowly tilted upward. The woman's smile proved most distracting. Griffin had to look to Caroline to gather his thoughts again.

"I am to take my mother to the theater tomorrow evening. If you ladies are not engaged elsewhere, I thought you might wish to join us."

"The theater?" Caroline said at the same moment Phoebe asked, "Which theater?"

"Covent Garden," he said, noting the way her eyes widened. His plan seemed to be working. "There will be a pantomime and then a comedy. *The Eccentric Lover*. Have either of you heard of it?"

Caroline started to shake her head, but Phoebe moved closer to the end of her seat.

"I have only just had it recommended to me," Phoebe said, her tone bright with excitement. "By a friend. I should very much like to go. I do not believe we are yet engaged anywhere else, are we Caroline?"

"I am afraid Joseph and I have already accepted a dinner invitation." Caroline tilted her head to the side, regarding her sister-in-law with care. Phoebe's shoulder slumped, and Griffin held his breath. It had been a gamble, to think they would have no plans on such short notice, but there was still a chance.

Phoebe's smile disappeared a moment before she seemed to remember herself under scrutiny. "Oh. That is a shame. Perhaps another time, Mr. Fenwick?"

Griffin did not get the chance to respond.

"Oh, Phoebe." Caroline giggled and took the younger woman's hand. "You need not come to a dinner full of strangers. I will make your excuses. If Mrs. Fenwick and Griffin will take you in their carriage, I believe you will be well chaperoned and looked after. There is no reason to miss a play you will likely enjoy."

Phoebe's warm brown eyes brightened, and she met Griffin's gaze with a most exuberant smile that caused his heart's tempo to pick up in speed. "I should very much like to attend with you, Mr. Fenwick, if you do not mind Caroline's absence."

He did not mind in the slightest. "Then I will come here for you tomorrow evening, Miss Kimball."

Tea arrived at that moment, and Caroline poured each of them a cup. They spoke of inconsequential things, of mutual friends, while Phoebe sat quietly nibbling upon a small cake. Strange, he had not thought her at all shy on previous occasions. But her mind may have turned to other matters, and Griffin had to hide his smile behind his cup when he saw Phoebe's hand reach for the book at her side. She laid her palm upon it, and a blush returned to her cheeks.

Griffin took his leave with a feeling of lightness he had never experienced. Never before had he looked forward to an evening enough to wish the present time away. With his mother as chaperone, Griffin would sit next to Phoebe for an entire evening's entertainment. If he was very lucky, he would move to the top of her list of suitors before the play ended.

CHAPTER 8

THE PLAY IS THE THING

To My Friend,

    Tonight I go to see the very play you have mentioned, and perhaps you will see me there. I am escorted by one of the gentlemen you named to me, Mr. Fenwick. He is acquainted with my sister-in-law and her family, so I have more than your reference to know he is a good man. But I do not believe he is a man with any interest in matrimony at present. Rather, I hope he will know the others you have presented.

    I find that I wonder if you and I are acquainted at all, sir. Perhaps you know my family. Though if that was so, why did you write to me a warning when you might have approached my brother? I confess that I am confused as to how you came to an awareness of my situation and interests. I understand why you must remain anonymous now, of course. We have exchanged enough letters to scandalize even the most lenient of chaperones.

    But would you give me a hint, even the very smallest hint, as to your identity? On my honor, I promise I have no wish to cause you shame or anything unpleasant. I am merely curious.

    Perhaps you will write to me after the play and tell me what you thought of the performance. I will happily share all my *thoughts with you, my friend. I must send this letter on its way to you and prepare for an evening of great enjoyment.*

Yours, etc.,

P.K.

Phoebe checked the arrangement of her hair once more in the parlor mirror. Mr. Fenwick would arrive at any moment to escort her to Covent Garden. She had eaten dinner alone, and early, in her room. Caroline and Joseph had left hours earlier, before she had even finished dressing for the evening.

She wore an amber cross and her bracelet, and red ribbons in her hair. Her gown was ivory with a red-net overlay that would shimmer in the soft gaslight of the theater. In her reticule she carried a red silk fan and Caroline's opera telescope. After smoothing her dress and checking again that she had all she needed, Phoebe paced from the window to the hearth.

Her stomach felt rather full of loose feathers, tickling her until she could not sit still. What made her nervous, she could not tell. There was the excitement of the play, of course. Perhaps in part it was due to the anticipation of an evening with a handsome gentleman—for Griffin was quite handsome, even if he was not a serious suitor. But the idea that her anonymous friend could be present, that she might see him and not even know, set her to fidgeting. But what if she *did* recognize him? Perhaps he would give her a secret sign, or come upon her in the theater corridor and she would simply *know* it was he?

"The Fenwick carriage has arrived, Miss Kimball." The

butler's pronouncement nearly made her leap out of her satin slippers.

"Oh. Thank you." She smiled shakily and went to the door which opened at the same moment she stepped into the foyer.

Griffin stepped inside, his customary grin in place, until the moment he spied her. His grin faltered, his eyes grew wider, and Phoebe hastily put her hand upon her stomach to calm the dratted feathers.

"Miss Kimball." He did not seem to know what else to say, as he simply stared at her. Phoebe's cheeks warmed beneath his rather fierce gaze.

"Mr. Fenwick. Is your mother waiting for us in the carriage?"

He jolted back into awareness, his smile appearing almost pasted on. "Yes. Of course. Here, allow me." He took her shawl from the butler and held it out to assist her.

"Thank you." Phoebe turned to allow him to lay it over her shoulders. Despite the layers of fabric between them, the warmth of his hands lingered a moment after he removed them from her arms.

He cleared his throat, and when Phoebe looked up she saw his good-natured grin had finally returned. "Shall we?" he asked, offering her his arm.

"Yes, please." Phoebe walked out the door upon his arm, and her eyes went to the very fine vehicle waiting in the street.

"My father decided to come as well," Griffin said, voice low. "Once he realized Caroline could not come. We have a box to ourselves, and he is not one to miss an evening in my mother's company if he can help it."

Phoebe tilted her head up to look at Griffin's rather

calm expression. He did not look as though he had just said something extraordinary. "Your father and mother enjoy one another's company that much?"

Griffin chuckled. "They adore one another, Miss Kimball." He paused outside the carriage and took her hand to help her in. He gave her fingers a gentle press. "You will see."

Phoebe entered the carriage and took her seat next to a woman of median age and a fine figure. The immediate welcome the woman gave, along with a warm smile, reminded Phoebe of Griffin at once.

Mrs. Fenwick's tone was as playful as her son's. "At last we meet you, Miss Kimball. Griffin has mentioned you so often these last several days that I confess myself most curious about you."

Griffin, who had barely sat down next to his father in the rear-facing seat, groaned. "Mother. You promised."

"Oh, pooh." His mother waved a hand at him. "Miss Kimball must know she is a lovely woman. I am certain she is used to the attention." Mrs. Fenwick gave Phoebe's hand a maternal pat. "Do not mind him, dear. Griffin is far too sensitive."

A giggle escaped Phoebe's lips, and she looked at Griffin in time to see him appear surprised.

Mr. Fenwick chuckled. "A pleasure to meet you, Miss Kimball. I do hope my wife and son will not drive you to distraction this evening. They both delight in teasing."

Griffin and his mother immediately protested that statement, amusing Phoebe enough that she relaxed in their company. An evening with such company promised entertainment, even if the play proved unamusing.

When they arrived at the theater, their carriage near the entrance, throngs of people already lined the walk and the steps to the entrance. The grand columns never failed to elicit admiration of its grandeur in Phoebe. When the original theater had burned down, though she had not yet been out in Society, she had mourned its loss.

Mr. and Mrs. Fenwick stepped out of the carriage first and waited arm-in-arm for their son to exit the vehicle. Griffin's shoes hit the pavement and he immediately turned back to her, his smile broad, and held out his gloved hand.

A thrill of excitement, like an electric bolt, went from Phoebe's fingertips to her toes when she took his hand. Such was her love for the theater, of course. The tingling sensation had nothing to do with the way Griffin's eyes gleamed with admiration. Though not a great beauty, Phoebe had enough self-assurance to call herself pretty. But to be the object of a gentleman's favorable assessment was rather enjoyable.

"Come, come. We need to get to our box." Mr. Fenwick led them forward with his head held high. He had to be nearing sixty years old, but he stood at the same height as his son.

"He is a spry old chap," Griffin murmured in her ear, as though he had read her thoughts. "I think the rest of us are lucky to keep up with him."

Phoebe's mind turned to her father, home at their country house tending to her mother. "You are fortunate to have parents in such good health that they actively seek an evening out with each other, and with you."

Griffin chuckled, a low sound she found she rather liked. "Come now, Miss Kimball. While I admit that they would both do very well on their own this evening, we will not pretend they are here for my sake at all. They both wished to meet you."

Her cheeks warmed and her stomach tightened into a knot. "Me? Oh dear. Why would I matter?"

They entered the theater where the lights blazed in wall sconces and a chandelier. It was louder inside, with people calling to one another and an excited hum grew into rumblings. The noise necessitated that Griffin draw closer, leaning down so that she felt his warm breath upon her neck when he spoke. "Meeting you is rather important to them, given that I have never before extended an invitation for a lady to accompany us to the theater."

She had to protest. It simply would not do that she interpret his remark as anything of importance. "You invited Caroline—"

"Only as an excuse to invite you, Miss Kimball."

Phoebe turned quickly to look at him, to measure the truth in his words, at the same moment someone bumped him from behind. Griffin moved forward, and their noses collided. Phoebe yelped and immediately put a hand to her stinging nose, while Griffin straightened and barked a protest at whoever had come up behind him.

Then he had her arm and pulled her along to the steps, but rather than go up as his parents had, he took her to the side where a lamp glowed in a wall sconce. He turned her toward the lamp, then his gloved fingers skimmed against her jaw, coaxing her to tip her face up toward him and the light.

He was studying her nose.

"Are you hurt, Miss Kimball?"

He had to stand close to do so, his stare rather intense with his eyebrows drawn down sharply and his lips pressed tightly together.

"It only stings a little." The unpleasant sensation had nearly entirely gone.

Never had Phoebe seen Griffin without a smile upon his face. He perpetually showed good humor, even in surprise. But all it took was one moment of concern for a more solemn expression to appear.

As handsome as Griffin was when he smiled—and as preferable as she found his wide grin to his frown—a more serious mien looked just as well upon him.

He stared down at her, not moving away, and Phoebe thought he meant to come closer—and she could not remember why that would be a bad thing.

Until someone laughed, loudly, breaking whatever trance Phoebe and Griffin had fallen under. He blinked as rapidly as she when he stepped back, looking over his shoulder. No one appeared to see them, to give any heed to them at all. Everyone was moving into the theater's entrances, backs to the little corner Griffin had found to tend to her.

Phoebe cleared her throat, then turned away from him. "We had better find your box. Your parents will wonder what became of us." At least they were in a public enough place that she need not worry about her reputation.

"You are right, of course. Miss Kimball." He offered his arm again, and she took it, avoiding looking up into his eyes.

For one wild moment, she had thought he might kiss her. While that ought to have disturbed, Phoebe found herself wondering instead if she would have liked it. The feathers returned to tickle her insides, and her cheeks warmed enough that she wished for her fan to cool them.

Griffin's parents were already seated in two chairs, with two more in front of them closer to the rail. Phoebe took her seat slowly, listening as Griffin made their excuses.

"We had a small mishap, but I see we have not missed so much as the pantomime."

"Have you heard anything about this play, Miss Kimball?" Mrs. Fenwick asked, her tone cheerful. "I was fortunate enough to see it performed more than a decade ago. I am most interested to see if it is as amusing as I remember."

"The story is about several couples making a hash of courtship." Mr. Fenwick took his wife's hand as he spoke. "Of course we will enjoy it. For it all ends happily enough."

Griffin at last sat down next to Phoebe, his smile returned to his lips. They were in a top box, to the right of the stage, and near the center of the room. Phoebe removed her small telescope from her reticule, along with her fan, and put the items upon the empty chair on her other side.

The lights flickered, and the people in the aisles of seats below quieted. Everything went quite dark. Griffin leaned close enough for his shoulder to brush hers. "Let me know if there is anything you require this evening, Miss Kimball. Anything at all."

Phoebe did not have time to reply before the orchestra began to play. As the man dressed as a fool put on his brief pantomime act, Phoebe's thoughts tumbled about the way he tumbled across the stage. She had not thought, when she first laid eyes upon Griffin Fenwick in Hyde Park, that he could be more than a fool himself. Performing foolish pranks and jests in front of Society, thumbing his nose at propriety.

Yet she could not think of any man of her acquaintance, save her relatives, who had treated her with such kind attentiveness. While his humor was not what she was used to, there was nothing inappropriate about it. Not really. He had never behaved as anything less than a gentleman when near her.

For some reason, he spoke often enough about her to make his parents curious. To ask her to an evening at the theater. It was enough to make her consider, to entertain the thoughts, that Griffin Fenwick considered courting her.

The audience's laughter filled the theater, and Phoebe forced a laugh as well. She laughed at herself. Griffin had proclaimed himself uninterested in marriage. She had heard it with her own ears. Her anonymous friend was wrong to put Griffin's name in his list. The only reason he showed her any consideration at all was due to his friendship with Caroline. Perhaps he still thought he must make up for his verbal blunder.

Yet during the third act of the play, after the intermission wherein she and Mrs. Fenwick laughed at the plights of the confused lovers, Griffin sat closer than before. He leaned down often to make observations about the characters that made her giggle most unbecomingly. He did not seem to mind.

And at the very end of the play, for a very brief moment, his hand covered hers when the hero at last confessed himself in love with the heroine.

CHAPTER 9

A FRIEND INDEED

To P.K.,

I did see you at the theater. You appeared most lovely in your gown, reminding me of cherry blossoms in the spring, or roses in the summer. Your companions were fortunate to have you in their box. When I took my eyes from the stage, it was always to seek you out. You seemed to have enjoyed the evening's entertainment, and I could not help but laugh when you laughed.

What thought you of Sir Francis? I rather wished I had the ability to throttle the character. Eleanor deserved someone far less reticent in telling her how he loved her. But that is the way of it at times; not everyone can wed someone deserving of their devotion.

I find I must address your curiosity now. You asked for a hint as to my identity. I fear I would choose poorly and send you on to an entirely wrong assumption. Or perhaps I would give you a hint that would reveal immediately who I am. Neither situation suits me at present.

Perhaps one day, in the future, I might tell you who I am. Until then, know that your letters are safe in my care. I have the greatest respect for you and for your family. When I wrote to you the very *first time, it was the only choice I had to make you aware of the scoundrel at your door.*

Tell me, did your Mr. Fenwick seem willing to introduce you to those other gentlemen I mentioned?

Your Friend

Phoebe sat in the parlor, waiting for Daphne Windham's arrival. Somehow, Daphne had contrived to come without her mother and only a maid for company. Thank goodness. What Phoebe wished to discuss was not for Mrs. Windham's ears. Mrs. Windham was terrible about keeping secrets, especially when they might be of use to her.

The latest letter written by her anonymous friend was in her sewing basket beneath the couch. She had already read through it several times, each time trying to puzzle out if there was any hidden meaning to any of the man's words. The first time she read it through, she blushed and smiled, feeling he paid her compliments and perhaps even flirted. Then she read it again and thought he pushed her toward Griffin. Another reading and she had nearly convinced herself that the writer cared not at all for her, only for propriety.

"I am being nonsensical," she said aloud.

"No one would ever accuse you of that, Phoebe. Except for perhaps those of us you convinced to swim in the pond at midnight." Daphne had arrived in the doorway, without Phoebe realizing she had even entered the house.

Phoebe rose and went to her friend, arms extended. "Daphne. Here you are at last. Oh, my dear, how are you?" They embraced more like sisters than friends and soon were upon the couch recounting the last week to each other. All the friends wrote fairly regularly, but with Daphne so near they had exchanged letters almost weekly.

"My parents are still trying to find a wealthy husband for me, but I am not interested in a mercenary marriage. I am still hoping for a love match. But things have grown much more complicated lately, what with…" Her voice trailed away, and her eyes lost focus.

A twist of worry made Phoebe lean forward. "With what?"

Daphne shook her head and a bright smile reappeared upon her face. "Nothing. I am certain everything will come to rights in the end." Phoebe nearly pressed her, but Daphne continued speaking. "Do tell me more about you, Phoebe. In your letter you made it sound like there was something rather particular you wished to discuss."

"There is." Phoebe chewed her bottom lip a moment, carefully watching Daphne. "Let us settle in with our refreshment first." Her friend remained silent while Phoebe poured out for them. It was only after the two of them were seated that Phoebe tried to work out how to begin.

Her friend appeared as calm as ever, sipping her tea and waiting patiently. While Phoebe had always been the one with a plan, Daphne had always provided a quiet and steady presence, usually with a smile upon her face. She had always been easy to confide in. But this confession bordered on scandalous.

"As you know, I have decided I must find a husband this Season. Someone suitable to my tastes, equal to my family in status."

"And someone you love," Daphne put in quickly. "As we all promised."

Phoebe looked away, clasping her hands together tightly in her lap. "At this point, I think we ought to agree that promise we made was very well and good for children. But as we are all adults now, and with varying situations in Society as in life, we must be more realistic."

Daphne sighed and set down her tea. "A year ago, I might have rejected that idea outright. But London has a way of making one doubt her own mind. Why is it that love is so difficult to find?"

Considering that Daphne had always seemed the one most determined to keep the promise they had made, Phoebe's heart ached for her friend's discovery that reality was not so romantic as they had dreamed it. Perhaps they would all come to that conclusion, in time. She studied her friend, trying to smile past her concerns. "I will continue to hope for the best for you, Daphne."

Her friend returned the gentle expression. "What is it you wish to tell me?"

Phoebe pulled in a careful breath. "What I wish to tell you is that in my pursuit of a suitor, I started to receive notes from a stranger. Someone who wishes to remain anonymous. But he has helped me more than once by informing me of things I had no way of knowing, and saving me from making mistakes by courting the wrong gentlemen."

Daphne blinked. "What do you mean, a stranger is writing you letters? How? And are you certain the stranger is a he?"

"I am. You can tell by his writing. And by the way he says things. Here. See for yourself." She reached under the couch and plucked the letter from the basket, handing it directly to Daphne.

Her friend gave her an odd look, then hurried to read the letter. Phoebe watched for a reaction, desperate to know how her friend interpreted the words penned by the unknown gentleman who had promised to help Phoebe.

When Daphne lowered the letter to her lap, she looked at Phoebe with wide eyes. "Honestly, reading this, it sounds as though the writer rather admires you and wishes to court you himself."

The relief which flooded Phoebe's mind caused a light laugh to escape her. "Oh, I am glad you think so. That is what I thought, too, when I read it. But then I was so worried—"

"Phoebe." Daphne stopped her, though her voice was hesitant. "You know nothing about him. He might be fifty years old with twelve children. He might even already be married."

The tightness returned to Phoebe's chest. "Yes. I had thought of that. I wondered if I ought to ask him, but then I think he would *know* what I suspected, or he would be insulted." Phoebe wrapped her arms around herself and leaned back, most unladylike, on the couch. "But he writes such charming letters. And every time I receive one, I cannot help but feel some excitement." Indeed, she could feel herself blushing just speaking about it.

Daphne sat back as well, eyeing Phoebe curiously. "Charming, you say? I suppose there is as much a chance of him being young and handsome as there is of him being fifty and married." She tugged restlessly on one of her red-brown curls. "Excitement and mystery are all well and good, I suppose. But you are taking care, aren't you? Not to be discovered?"

"I will not be discovered." Phoebe sat up at once. "I have been very discreet, as has the gentleman. He has never even approached me—"

"That you know of," Daphne corrected. Then tapped the paper with one finger. "What about this Mr. Fenwick? It sounds as though your gentleman likes him. Did you enjoy his company at the play?"

Phoebe waved a hand dismissively. "I always enjoy Griffin's—Mr. Fenwick's company."

Daphne's eyes lit up at Phoebe's slip of the tongue. "Griffin. That is his given name, yes?" Phoebe narrowed her eyes, but Daphne kept talking. "It seems to me that if your anonymous *friend* pointed you toward Mr. Fenwick, and Mr. Fenwick seems to like spending time with you, you ought to pay more attention to him than to someone who will not even tell you his real name." Daphne nodded once, firmly, to punctuate her argument.

With a sigh, Phoebe accepted the letter from her friend's hand and turned it over in her own. The rampant lion glared up at her from the red wax seal.

"I do enjoy Mr. Fenwick's company. Last evening, at the theater, he was so attentive and kind." Without thinking, she reached up to touch the tip of her nose, but hastily lowered her hand again to her lap. "But he as good as told me that he has no interest in marriage at present."

Daphne pursed her lips and narrowed her eyes at Phoebe. "I am certain most men say that up until the moment they meet the lady who interests them above all others. It is rather like showing one's hand in a game of Whist. He does not wish you to know whether he holds a trump or a useless deuce."

A laugh burst from Phoebe, and it only took Daphne a moment to join in with her own giggles. Phoebe shook a finger at her friend. "Your mother would not at all like your Whist metaphor."

Daphne's cheeks colored, but her eyes danced. "I know. But I trust you will not tell her." She relaxed, and fixed Phoebe with a look of concern. "You are one of my dearest friends. I want you to be happy, but I also want you to be careful. Perhaps you ought to suggest a meeting. Nothing clandestine. Just a walk in the park where you both sit on the same bench or carry the same book. You would not even have to speak. But you would see him and know at once whether there is more there than a friendship."

The wisdom in her friend's suggestion rendered Phoebe silent for several moments as she thought it over.

"And," Daphne added with a crooked smile, "perhaps give this Mr. Fenwick a chance. Since he was so 'attentive and kind' last evening.'"

"Perhaps I will." Phoebe turned the note in her hands over again, hiding the lion from sight. "Now. I want to hear more about you. What plans have you this coming week? Perhaps we can contrive to attend the same parties for once."

CHAPTER 10

OUT OF SORTS

S ince the night of the play, Griffin had exchanged several notes with Phoebe. The first she had obviously written after their evening together as it was full of her thoughts on the play and nothing else. She did not ask for more hints, which was a relief. But she also did not mention the name Griffin Fenwick again.

He wrote a response, concluding his thoughts on the play, and then sharing thoughts on a book he had read. Of course, Griffin mentioned it in the anonymous letter because he had seen the book upon the table in her house when he had visited. It was the book she had put the anonymous letter inside. The second volume of a novel called *Sense and Sensibility*.

They exchanged a note each on the subject of the book, Griffin smiling over every word she penned, before he finally went somewhat mad.

Griffin needed to see Phoebe again. In person. And he had not been able to think of another excuse for arriving at her door, unless he finally admitted his interest in courtship.

"That would be the reasonable thing to do," he muttered to himself as he entered his family's townhouse. But making his interest known in such a way would put pressure upon it, he well knew, and cause those with critical eyes to watch and wait and comment on the relationship.

"Griffin, darling, is that you?" His mother called from the drawing room. "Do come here, son, and tell me where you have been the last two days."

Entering the room, Griffin saw his father seated in a chair with his feet on a stool. He looked over the book he was reading and smiled at his son. "Fair warning, all your mother really wants to know is whether you have seen Miss Kimball of late."

Griffin's mother embraced him, then shook her finger at her husband. "Do not pretend I am the only one who is curious. You have been speaking of her as much as I have."

Though it somewhat alarmed him to know his parents had speculated on his relationship with Phoebe, Griffin decided it would be better if he were merely amused. He fixed his grin upon his face, kissed his mother on the cheek, then flopped inelegantly into the chair near his father.

"What do you think of Miss Kimball, Father?"

"Same as I did after the play. She is a lovely, lively young woman." Mr. Fenwick closed his book and took off his spectacles. "Ask me what I think of *you,* Son."

Raising his eyebrows, Griffin obeyed. "What do you think of me, Father?"

"I think," his father said slowly, drawing each word out with some severity, "that you have avoided us these two days past because *you* like Miss Kimball excessively."

"I concur," Mrs. Fenwick said shortly. She walked to the mantel, hands clasped behind her back. "You have never shown such interest in a young lady before, Griffin."

Shifting uncomfortably in his seat would give too much away. Instead, he tipped his head back and looked up at the ceiling. "Miss Kimball is lovely, I grant you. She has a lively mind, as you said. I find her to be intelligent and a witty conversationalist."

"Then what keeps you from coming to know her better?" Mr. Fenwick asked, spectacles and book still in hand. "We raised you to recognize such things in others so that you would seek out the companionship of friends, and eventually a wife, with those fine qualities."

Griffin considered the plastered ceiling with a grimace. "I do not think she views me entirely favorably. I am afraid our first introduction made me appear a fool, and I have hardly seen her since without there arising one problem or another. The theater was my first successful interaction with her since we met." He swung his gaze down to his parents, his mother standing behind his father's chair. "I rather wish for that impression to settle upon her before I try again."

"And in the meantime, some cleverer chap will step in and—" His father's unhelpful pronouncement was interrupted when Mrs. Fenwick covered her husband's mouth with one hand.

"Your father made inquiries," she said. "He quite likes what he has learned about the Kimballs."

Mr. Fenwick took his wife's hand, kissed it, then moved it to rest upon his shoulder. "Your mother made inquiries, too. We both like what she has learned about the young lady."

Griffin looked from one parent's knowing smile to

the other. "I suppose that is a good thing?" He did not like the way they stared at him, as though they had something else to share but thought it far too delicious at present. "But what is this? You have never pushed me, either of you, to take a wife. Why all the interest now?"

"Because of your interest, obviously," his father said.

His mother made a sound Griffin would never dare call a snort. "And because all our friends have grandchildren."

Griffin's mouth popped open. *Grandchildren?* That is putting the cart before the horse, is it not?"

Husband and wife exchanged another look, then his mother sighed. "I was afraid we would encounter this reluctance. I forbid you to get our hopes up about a daughter-in-law, Griffin."

"I have not—"

"And that is why," she said, speaking over him, "I have invited Miss Kimball and her family to dinner this evening."

Griffin nearly fell out of his chair. "You have?"

"Indeed." She smiled and lifted her chin. "Be here at seven this evening, please. We need you to decide if we should pin our hopes on this young woman or if we ought to settle in for an even longer wait."

Griffin opened and closed his mouth several times, then he finally laughed and rose from his chair. "Mother, you are an angel." He crossed the room and kissed her cheek. "Father, I will see you this evening." He shook his father's hand, then turned and went to the door.

"But Griffin," his mother called. "You only just arrived."

"I have things to see to before tonight. Thank you, Mother." He left the house with a lighter heart. His *mother* had found a way for him to see Phoebe, without forcing him to reveal his intentions.

He made his way to Berkeley Square, with the hope of finding another note waiting for him. To have the pleasure of a letter and Phoebe's company on the same evening would put him in the best of moods for days to come.

To My Friend,

I have enjoyed our exchange of letters this past week. I am delighted to know you have read so many of my favorite novels. But lest you suspect I fill my head with nothing but modern fiction, I will promise you that I have enjoyed many a Shakespearian play and sonnet, too. Of course, most of my reading is quite frivolous by scholarly standards.

This evening I go to dinner with the Fenwick family. I know Mr. Griffin Fenwick is a favorite of yours, from the list you gave me. Why is that? How well do you know him, or any of the men on that list, to recommend them?

I confess, I have not sought out anyone else you named. I find I would much rather come to know you more. You call yourself my friend, but how can that be, when we are restricted to letter writing and nothing more? I have confided in one of my closest friends, a woman I have known since childhood, about our letters. She has given me the best of advice.

I should like to see you. We need not meet in secret, or indeed speak a word to one another. I thought we might both go for a walk the day after tomorrow. In Hyde Park, at noon. It is not the fashionable hour, so there will be few people about. There is a particular tree near the Serpentine—it is old and bent, with one branch forming an arch all the way to the ground. If you will walk to that tree, and carry any object of red, I will know it is you.

We need not speak, if you do not wish it. But it is unfair that you know me so well, that you have seen me and known it is to me you write, and I know not if I have ever glimpsed you.

Please say you agree.

Yours,

P.K.

Phoebe followed Caroline and Joseph into the Fenwick townhouse. It was not far distant from their own. Merely a street over.

The uncle in Parliament would not be present, for which she was grateful. There was no one to impress. The Fenwicks had proved most kind the night of the play. And Griffin— he seemed to like her well enough.

Phoebe put her hand over the red-bead bracelet, drawing in a deep breath. She wore an ivory gown and her blue-green shawl, a red ribbon in her hair the only thing which matched her friends' bracelet. Even if there was no one to impress, she hoped at least one person that evening would think she looked pretty.

"Mr. Kimball, Caroline, it is such a pleasure to have you both with us." Mrs. Fenwick kissed Caroline upon the cheek after they curtsied and bowed to one another. Then she turned with a wide smile that looked very much like her son's and extended a hand to Phoebe. "And you, Miss Kimball. I am simply delighted you could come. I so enjoyed getting to know you at the theater."

"Thank you for inviting me," Phoebe said, then her eyes went to where the older Mr. Fenwick stood. The invitation had said their son would be present, yet he did not greet the guests with his parents?

"Griffin has not yet arrived," Mr. Fenwick said, and she blushed when she looked back to him. At least he seemed to be telling all three guests, and not just Phoebe. "It is not like him to be late, so I am certain whatever keeps him is pressing." He gestured to the steps leading to the next floor. "Caroline, permit me to escort you to the parlor. And do tell me how your father is doing, spending all his time in Bath."

Joseph offered his arm to Mrs. Fenwick, leaving Phoebe to follow behind all of them. She hesitated a moment, feeling somewhat unsettled. The disappointment she felt at Griffin's absence, even if it was temporary, surprised her.

Phoebe's hand went to the bannister, and she took her first step upon the stairs, at the same moment the front door opened. Startled, Phoebe turned around with her heart in her throat.

With hat in hand, Griffin entered the house. He had not seen her yet. He handed his things to the footman. "Thank you, Clarkson. Have the other guests arrived?"

"Yes, Mr. Griffin. They have only just gone upstairs, sir."

"Thank you."

He turned and saw her. His eyes widened, and his warm smile appeared. In three long strides Griffin was at her side, extending his hand to her. She took it without thinking, and he bowed over her bracelet as though she were a queen.

"Miss Kimball," he said. "It seems my timing is quite perfect. I have caught you alone."

Phoebe's lips parted, and she looked up to see that everyone else had disappeared. Even the footman had gone, leaving her alone in the entry hall with Griffin. She looked back at him, but rather than feel startled at being alone with a man, relief made her laugh. "So you have, sir. If you have anything of a clandestine nature to reveal, now is the time to do so."

His smile faltered, and Phoebe hastily spoke on. "Not that I think you are a secretive person, Griff—Mr. Fenwick. I only meant to jest."

His congenial expression returned, though more subdued. "Griff. Hm. I rather like that. Are we acquainted well enough yet that I can insist you call me by that name and nothing else?" His voice was warm, but she could not call it more than friendly.

"Oh, I am afraid we have not known each other nearly long enough. Perhaps in a decade." She attempted to keep the levity in her tone, though her heart raced. "And only if your wife does not mind." Phoebe's heart abruptly stopped, then everything above her shoulders went hot as she blushed. "I did not mean to suggest—that is—"

Griffin laughed, not unkindly, and offered her his arm. "It is only fair you should bungle a word or two, Miss Kimball, given how I have already had my turn at such a mistake."

Though mortified, Phoebe took his arm. "I am somewhat out of sorts this evening, I suppose." They started up the stairs, walking more slowly than necessary. Phoebe could not mind when it meant a few more moments to try to understand the man at her side. She did enjoy his company and simply being near him made her heart lighter.

"I am sorry to hear that. I hope you are not troubled by anything serious." He sounded sincere, and when she looked at him from the side of her eye she saw his brow had drawn down, as though with real concern.

"Not troubled. Distracted, only. But now that you are here to keep me entertained, I will endeavor to be more focused." She tightened her fingers about his arm a little, hoping to offer him her reassurance.

Griffin's smile was fleeting. "Entertained. Yes, I suppose I am rather talented at doing that." They made the landing and went through the open doors to the parlor before Phoebe could think what else to say to restore his cheer.

"Ah, there is Miss Kimball. And look, she has found our missing son." Mr. Fenwick had a heartiness to him that brought a smile back to his son's face, and Phoebe's worry eased. Perhaps Griffin had private matters distracting him, too.

CHAPTER 11

REVELING CONVERSATION

Though Griffin had looked forward to Phoebe's company all the day long, her letter had thrown him off balance. To see her thoughts affected enough that she stumbled over her words to him on the stair actually concerned him. While he had attempted to put himself forward as a suitor gradually, with more caution than he normally exercised in any part of his life, he had also managed to create his own rival.

Given what Phoebe had said in her letter, and had implied in her desire to meet her "friend" at last, she had romantic interest in the anonymous writer.

What would she do when she discovered they were one and the same man?

"Mr. Kimball, I do hope you are treating our Caroline well. I must say, she appears even happier now than when you last visited us in Essex." His mother smiled from her place at one end of the table, fondly taking in Caroline's blush and grin.

"With good reason, Mrs. Fenwick," Joseph Kimball said, laying his hand upon his wife's. They sat most informally that evening, given the friendships between them. He had the same coloring as his sister, but quite a different structure. "Do tell them, my dear. I know you wish to do so."

Caroline's blush deepened.

Griffin chuckled. "Come, Caroline. We must know what brings you such joy." Perhaps they had purchased a town home of their own, or planned to host a ball, or—

"We are increasing the size of our family by one," Caroline said, her eyes glowing with joy.

Fenwick's mother gasped and then raised her glass. "To my dearest Caroline Kimball. You will be a most excellent mother." Everyone raised their glasses, and after drinking to Caroline's health, Griffin's father added his own kind words.

"Your mother and father must be very pleased. This will be their first grandchild by you, of course, but how many have your brothers and sisters produced by now?"

Caroline laughed, but Griffin sunk back in his chair when his mother gave him a knowing glance. "There are six others to be cousins to our future child."

Griffin turned to look at Phoebe only to find her staring at him, with a rather perplexed expression upon her face.

"Do you not like children, Mr. Fenwick?" she asked quietly.

Dash it all, her list. He quickly recovered himself. "I have a great fondness for them, actually. When Caroline's nieces and nephews descend upon their grandparents, who are my country neighbors, you will remember, I am always quick to lead them in their games. I was only surprised, just then. Caroline is younger than I am by seven years. It is strange to think of her as a mother."

Phoebe's eyes lightened. "Ah, it is as I said before. You are a very old man. All of eight-and-twenty *years*, even though you are unfortunate in the number of birthdays you have enjoyed."

Griffin laughed at last, relieved that she would jest with him. When she teased, there was a spark in her eyes he rather loved. The way her lips tipped upward when she spoke quickly, with wit, drew him in, too.

The conversation shifted, and Phoebe rejoined it with gusto. Her dark curls brushed across her cheek on occasion, and Griffin's hand itched to brush them away so he might see her eyes better. The topic of conversation turned to books.

"I have only recently finished reading a novel by a lady author," Mrs. Fenwick said, and Griffin stiffened. "My son encouraged me to read it, which surprised me. Griffin will read many a first chapter but only continue if the book is excellent, of course, so I knew he must have enjoyed it. What was that book called, Griffin?"

His throat had closed. His correspondence over the last three days with Phoebe had included mention of the same book of which his mother spoke.

Mrs. Fenwick tapped her finger upon the table as she thought. "Oh, yes. *Sense and Sensibility.* Isn't that a lovely title?"

"Oh, I have read it, too. I finished the last volume only last week." Phoebe turned to Griffin, her eyebrows high. "What did you think of the book, Mr. Fenwick? You must have enjoyed it to recommend it to your mother."

Trapped. He had utterly trapped himself. What opinions could he give that the anonymous letter writer had not already shared? He looked to his mother, but found she watched him with a hopeful gleam in her eye. She wished for him to have this conversation with Phoebe on his own.

His words came out strangled. "I did enjoy it." Everyone at the table now stared at him, waiting for more. Why could not a servant drop a platter or something else distracting occur? A hurricane, perhaps. "I found the plight of the sisters most compelling. And though I began the book with full sympathy for the younger sister—Marianne—at its end I had a great deal more respect for Elinor."

His father and Joseph Kimball stared at him as though he had just announced himself bound for the Americas. Reading a book written by a lady might not suit most men, but the writing had been quite good. And Phoebe had recommended it. He had wanted, very much, to know what she liked and why.

Phoebe nodded, her gaze turning thoughtful. She must think it strange that he and her mysterious friend had read the same book. Or perhaps not. It had become a rather popular novel.

When she looked at him again, her eyes studied him. "I rather felt for Elinor during the whole of the novel. As practical as she was, the plans she tried to make, it must have been difficult to have everyone about her constantly undoing her careful work."

"It is impossible to plan everything, though," he said.

She lowered her chin and glanced away, her cheeks turning pink. "So I am learning." She gave him such a look at that moment, her eyes warm and soft, her smile delicate and almost uncertain, that his heart twisted. He would give himself away if he lingered upon how she looked. His heart was hers for the taking.

"What else do you enjoy reading?" Griffin asked,

desperate to change the topic from the novel they had written about in their notes. They were at a dinner table with his family and hers. It was not the time to stare at her like a besotted calf.

"Oh, I cannot think you and I have many more favorite books in common," she demurred, lifting her fork with some haste. Perhaps she had sensed the danger, too.

Griffin relaxed. They both wished to leave the dangerous waters. The others at the table had continued on another topic of conversation, leaving the two of them to murmur quietly to each other. "I imagine we might. Most of my reading is quite frivolous, too."

Phoebe's fork fell from her hand to clatter upon the plate, then slid completely off onto her lap. She yelped and jumped to her feet, but the food upon the fork had already made a streak of color down her dress.

Griffin rose, mouth agape. He realized too late what he had done. Her letter.

"Of course, most of my reading is quite frivolous by scholarly standards."

He had thought on it and responded as though she had spoken the words to him rather than written to the anonymous him. If she was not suspicious before, she certainly would be now. But perhaps not. Coincidences happened.

His mother stood too, napkin in hand. "Oh, dear girl. Here, let me help with that. Come, right this way." She took Phoebe's arm and led her from the dining room, obviously to tidy her up.

Just before the door closed upon them, Phoebe looked back, her eyes as wide and large as a full moon.

She knew.

"Most of my reading is quite frivolous, too."

Phoebe had never admitted to having such habits, using such words, to anyone before she had written that letter. When Griffin had said that single word, *frivolous*, everything in her mind had come together. By the time his mother had finished helping her clear the stain, and then the damp, from her dress, Phoebe had a clear picture in her mind of what had happened.

Griffin had introduced her to the gambler, Mr. Milbourne, before understanding why she wished to meet him. As a favor to Caroline, and perhaps out of guilt for performing the introduction, he had written that first note. And he had been present when she spoke with Mr. Peter Carew, so he had seen the shift in her interest and had warned her away again. She had mentioned loving the theater in a letter, and then Griffin had invited her to see a play. He even dared write, anonymously, to tell her he had seen her present. She had shared a favorite book, and then Griffin had read it and given it to his mother to read, too.

That very day, she had written and asked to meet him, only for them to have dinner together. Griffin was her mysterious friend. He had to be. Everything aligned perfectly.

And I was too stupid to see it.

Mrs. Fenwick surveyed Phoebe's gown again. "There we are. No one would ever know. Come, let us go back to the table. It is nearly time for dessert."

"Yes. Thank you." Phoebe followed her hostess as slowly as she could. What was she to say, or do, when she put eyes upon the man again?

What had he been thinking, writing her so many letters? Even putting forth his own name as a suitor! And to think she had been halfway in love with the letter writer, and certainly rather smitten by Griffin himself.

When she entered the dining room, she immediately lowered her eyes. What if she looked at him and saw laughter in his eyes? He had to know she had discovered the secret at last. Surely, he knew, and thought her a dull, foolish girl to have not realized it sooner. Perhaps he had even been laughing at her all along.

Pressure at the back of her eyes indicated that tears would come on, if she allowed it. But Phoebe pushed back the desire to cry.

"Is everything all right, Phoebe?" Joseph asked, his brotherly concern not as comforting as usual. He knew nothing of her plight. He could not help her.

Lowering herself into her seat, she looked across the table to her brother. "Yes, of course. Dear me, I do apologize for that interruption. I will not be so clumsy again." She would not look at Griffin. Not for a thousand pounds did she want to meet his gaze and read his thoughts in his eyes. They sat so near, if he wanted, he could lean over and touch her, yet all she felt was his gaze upon her.

The conversation resumed around her, and if anyone wondered at her silence, they likely thought it an effect of her embarrassment.

She did not want to be right. If her charming friend with his witty letters that served to cheer her and distract her, and Griffin Fenwick who acted foolish and sincere at different moments, were the same man, what did that say about him? What did that mean for her growing feelings toward—well, either of them?

If Griffin had received her letter from that day, he knew of her desire to meet the letter-writer.

Phoebe winced when Mr. Fenwick spoke his son's name.

"Griffin, were you not telling us about your plan to tour the old churches of London? It does not sound like an activity for one such as myself, but perhaps these younger people might be interested in joining you." He looked pointedly in Phoebe's direction.

"I do not intend to see them all at once," Griffin's pleasant tenor said from beside her, sounding as relaxed as ever. Oh, what a clever actor he was. "But I thought I would begin with All-Hallows-by-the-Tower. Situated that close to the oldest buildings in London, most of those I have talked to agree it is the oldest Christian church in the city." He shifted in his chair, but Phoebe refused to look at him. "Then St. Helen's and St. Giles."

"That sounds rather delightful." Caroline's eyes fairly glittered with excitement as she turned to Phoebe. "What do you think? Ought we to form part of Griffin's expedition? Exploring old churches would be a pleasant diversion after all the teas and parties. I know you prefer quiet to such noisy occasions."

What was Phoebe supposed to say? The noisy occasions were where women found husbands. She needed them. But Caroline's expression, hopeful and sly at once, indicated she thought Griffin a suitable exchange for all the bachelors at musicals and salons.

Phoebe looked to Joseph, her expression pleading.

"I think it sounds like a most excellent undertaking. I will attend myself. Our family prefers small, private gatherings to the more boisterous assemblies." Joseph had misinterpreted her look entirely, thinking she needed encouragement rather than a rescue.

"Miss Kimball?" Oh, no.

Phoebe slowly turned toward him, bracing herself for his deceitful grin.

Instead, she found his dark eyes pleading with her. His chin was tucked close to his chest, his eyes wide. When he spoke, she caught the slight rasp to his voice, though she doubted the others heard. "Would you accompany me to All-Hallow's? If you enjoy the outing, you might help me plan the next."

Phoebe lowered her head, uncertainty creeping over her like a chill. "Of course, Mr. Fenwick. Name the day."

She looked up at Caroline to find her sister-in-law with lips pressed flat and eyebrows drawn together. "Lovely," she said, then abruptly turned to Mrs. Fenwick and changed the topic of conversation entirely.

Griffin leaned close, voice low. "Miss Kimball, if you will allow me to explain—"

"Not now." She shivered and took up the new fork that had been placed on the table in her brief absence. She stabbed at a carrot, rather wishing she could stab at Griffin instead. Her humiliation was quite complete; the moment dinner finished she pleaded a headache.

Somehow, she made it out the door without saying another word to Griffin and avoided his gaze almost entirely. A man such as he, known for tricks and frivolity, could never have meant for their correspondence to mean as much as it had meant to her.

CHAPTER 12

BOTHERATION

D iscarding one letter after another, Griffin did not sleep. With his parents' words of concern ringing in his ears, he left their home for his rented rooms in something of a daze. With one sentence, he had ruined all his own plans.

Not that he had actually decided how to tell Phoebe he had been the one writing her anonymously. But he had started working on a plan. Almost. Mostly he had at least started thinking about it. When Phoebe's letter arrived asking to meet, something cold and icy, and rather like dread, grew in his chest.

"Turf and thunder," he muttered, tearing yet another letter to pieces. "Botheration." Truly, the situation merited more colorful language, but Griffin had no desire to add to his sins, at present.

Dawn crept into the room through the window, with him slumped in a chair before the embers of a fire. Cream-colored balls of paper were scattered about the room, or torn to bits and laying about like forgotten snowflakes.

"It shouldn't matter this much." He addressed his

comment to his stockinged feet. He'd kicked his shoes off and tossed his cravat over a chair at some point in the night. But the sheer panic with which he had written and scratched out an explanation for what he had done, for writing her and then deceiving her, proved that he could not cast his worries aside. He needed to ask himself a different question entirely. "Why does it matter this much?"

He had begun to consider courtship, and to consider what it might mean to enter into a formal commitment with Phoebe. But he'd hesitated in declaring such intentions. He had never courted anyone, because that meant making plans. Making plans hinted at a level of seriousness he had never felt quite prepared to accept. There would always be more time, another year, and plenty of women in England to consider.

Except for the last fortnight, he had only thought of Phoebe. He had laughed over her letters, admired her determination, and found her irresistibly intelligent and beautiful. He wanted to be near her, to come to know her better.

The last letter she had written him, before the fiasco of a dinner, she had asked to meet her anonymous friend. Perhaps he could convince her to meet him, still. Rather than explain in another letter. If he visited her home, the chances of them having a private audience were slim.

But if they met in the park, perhaps he could make things better.

He went to the curtains in his room, already open enough to allow a trickle of sunlight inside. He threw them open, wincing a bit. Then he took the edge of his desk and pulled it into the light. He had used all the

SALLY BRITTON

paper, but he found a piece he could trim down and
uncrumpled it on the flat surface.

Griffin chewed on his bottom lip, tapping his fingers
with the pen between them upon the desk. Then he
wrote.

To P.K.,

I understand that you are upset. I understand if you are angry.
But please, will you give me the chance to explain? We could meet,
as you suggested, at the tree in Hyde Park. I will be there.

Please come, as I remain, with my whole heart,
Your Friend

He sealed the note, the shortest he had ever written
Phoebe. The rampant lion appearing rather angry with
him.

Griffin found his cravat and tied it on rather sloppily,
then went in search of his shoes. The flower girl would be
there even that early. She had an entire cart of flowers in
the mornings, so grand houses might put flowers upon
ladies' breakfast trays and upon dining tables.

He flew out the door, uncaring that his appearance
might startle anyone of his class who saw him. The only
person whose opinion mattered was the recipient of his
note.

Phoebe stayed in bed as long as possible. She had not
slept much. Mostly she had tossed about in bed, trying to
recall every word she had written to her anonymous
friend. Had there been anything truly embarrassing?

Anything that would compromise her standing in Society besides the letters themselves?

Not that she thought Griffin would attempt to expose her in any way. Not intentionally.

She pulled a pillow over her face, ignoring the sounds of life outside her window. "I cannot trust *anything* he said. Because he lied."

Another part of her mind argued that her statement was false. Griffin had never spoken or written a falsehood. She had reread all his letters in the middle of the night, then folded them up and retied them in the red ribbon.

Even without the lying, Griffin had deceived her. What she could not understand was why he had kept writing once he had accomplished his purpose of warning her, or why he had continued to try to see her, in the park, and then escorting her to the play.

Her aching heart rather hoped he still wanted...something.

A knock on her bedroom door made her groan, then cast her pillow aside. "Who is there?"

"Caroline."

Phoebe pushed herself up in bed, pushing a few strands of hair that had come loose in the night behind her ears. "Come in."

The door opened, and Caroline came in with a maid behind her, carrying a breakfast tray. "You must eat, dear, even if you feel poorly. I have some tea with honey and lemon, and here is toast and some lemon cake." Another maid entered, holding a vase full of scarlet roses. "Oh, and someone sent you flowers. There is a note." The maids put their burdens on the dressing table, curtsied, and left.

Phoebe stared at the flowers from her place in bed, her

heart picking up speed until it reminded her of a galloping horse.

"Thank you, Caroline." Phoebe slid from between her sheets and went to the flowers. A note had been left tucked inside the stems. She pulled the paper out and went to the window, holding it up to the light.

The rampant lion upon the seal challenged her, glaring fiercely from the wax. She swallowed.

"It is kind of Griffin to send you flowers," Caroline said.

Phoebe nearly dropped the letter, but instead pressed it to her racing heart and turned to her sister-in-law. "How do you know it's from Griff—Mr. Fenwick?"

Caroline sat in Phoebe's chair near the hearth, tucking her legs beneath her. "The seal. His family has used the rampant lion for years. They have two statues like that, guarding the gate of their country estate."

Phoebe swallowed, then opened the note. She read it over twice in just a few seconds. The brevity in his words gave away nothing. Yet, she found herself relieved he had not attempted to explain, or make excuses, upon the paper. She folded it up and winced when she saw Caroline's expectant expression.

"He hopes I recover and that he will see me soon. Nothing else."

"Of course not. It would be inappropriate to say anything else." Caroline's eyes twinkled merrily. "Although I have heard a rumor that there have been a few letters with this seal coming into the house before."

Phoebe's cheeks blazed with heat, then she went cold all over. "Who said such a thing?" She laughed, the sound weak and unconvincing to her own ears.

Caroline's grin widened. "Very loyal and honest

servants. But never you fear, darling. I have nothing to say on the matter. I trust you. I have always known you to be practical, and Griffin is a gentleman for all that he behaves ridiculously at times."

Phoebe swallowed and nodded tightly. "Thank you. For not saying anything."

"I did sense that something was amiss between the two of you last evening. I do hope whatever happened will not cause a permanent wedge between you. He is a good friend of mine, do not forget." Caroline rose, and her face went pale. "If you will excuse me. I am afraid my own breakfast has not entirely agreed with me." She put a hand over her abdomen. "Actually, might I have one of your slices of toast to nibble at?"

Phoebe hastily picked up a square of bread and handed it to her sister-in-law.

"Thank you." Caroline took a small bite, forced a smile, and hastily left the room.

As much as her sister-in-law wished to help, her delicate condition had rather limited her ability to do much of late aside from rest and avoid becoming sick after every bite of food.

The roses caught her eye, and she bent to inhale their lovely scent. Red roses. A rather intimate offering, even if there was a liberal scattering of white carnations with them. She considered the flowers, then the note.

Did he deserve the chance to explain? Perhaps. But whether he did or not, Phoebe knew her own curiosity would drive her to be in the park the next day. She needed to hear what he had to say.

Phoebe opened the small box upon her dressing table and drew out the red-bead bracelet. Her friends might offer her advice, were they present. But there was no time to solicit it now. At least she had the bracelet, and the encouragement it represented.

Daphne, Marah, Lavinia, and Isabel, would all tell her the same thing. If she cared about Griffin Fenwick, and if there was any possibility that he had come to care for her, she had better meet with him.

Her heart approved the plan.

If only she did not have to wait an entire day to find out what Griffin had to say.

CHAPTER 13

A BEGINNING

The head of the Serpentine was actually quite narrow and properly called the Long Water. But hardly anyone took the time to remember that the lake boasted two different names for its different forms. Griffin arrived early, though he knew precisely which tree Phoebe had meant in her letter.

She had not written him after he sent the flowers or the note entreating her to meet him. What were the chances of her coming? Finding a chaperone to accompany her to the park, explaining why she wished to be present in the middle of the day rather than at the more conventional times, might prove difficult.

The gray clouds above, while not precisely threatening, might keep her away, too. Hyde Park was terribly deserted for such pleasant April weather.

He paced beneath the tree branches for a time before realizing he only added to his agitation with each step. So instead, and without a care for who saw him, Griffin sat down on the grass directly beneath the arching limb. He stared out over the water, watching a pair of swans glide slowly across the pond.

Griffin took his hat off and put it on the grass by his side. He drew up his knees and folded his arms, considering what he would say when Phoebe arrived. How did he explain himself? He could justify his first note to her, perhaps. But not all those which came after. Not really. He ought to have written Caroline to issue the warning about Richard Milbourne. Then dropped the matter entirely.

But he couldn't. Because every time he thought of Phoebe, thought of writing to her, hoping to catch sight of her, he found he wanted more. More of her words, her time, her conversation.

He scrubbed one hand through his hair before he remembered he wanted to look his best. He tried to press it back down into the style his valet had recommended, but gave up with a sigh.

All Griffin could give Phoebe by way of explanation was the truth.

He ought to have watched the paths but given that he did not expect Phoebe to come—not really, because why would she wish to give him even another moment of her time after his trickery?—it seemed better to watch the swans and birds.

A horse nickered behind him. Griffin did not turn. It could be anyone riding along the nearly deserted paths.

But then he heard her voice.

"If you will stay with the animals, Thompson, just there. Yes. I should like to take a moment and walk."

"As you say, miss," a young male voice said.

Griffin slowly rose to his feet, then turned to see Phoebe upon the path. A groom held two horses, and he made a point of not watching Phoebe approach Griffin.

He swallowed, squaring his shoulders and preparing to accept whatever she wished to say to him. If she railed, accused, stormed at him, he deserved it.

Phoebe wore a red riding habit, with silver epaulets, and a black hat with a red band. She looked rather like a feminine soldier marching toward him. Her red bracelet showed between the sleeve of her riding coat and the black wrist-length glove she wore.

Her eyes were not upon him, but upon the ground, until she stood only a few feet away from him. Then she looked up, her brown eyes full of questions. And pain.

"I am here," she said, voice soft. "To meet my mysterious friend."

Griffin swallowed and reached for his hat, only to realize he had left it upon the ground. He curled his hand into a loose fist instead, tapping it against his thigh. "Good afternoon, Miss P. K."

Phoebe stared at him, her lips pressed together tight, and her face rather pale. Then she licked her lips, looking away. "Why did you not tell me who you were?"

He must be honest. Make no excuses. Only explain. "When I wrote those first letters, you did not seem to like me much. I thought it best to remain anonymous, so you would not discard my words as those of a fool."

Her eyes darted upward, her lips parted in surprise. "A fool?"

He shrugged and tipped his head to one side, trying for a smile. "I am fairly certain that was your opinion of me. At least at first. And here I have proved it by creating this uncomfortable situation for you."

Phoebe stepped closer to him, her expression still neutral. "Perhaps at first, I did not recognize that you were a gentleman of wit as well as folly. But the more I saw you, I found myself rather hoping to be friends."

Griffin lowered his gaze to the ground between them. "I hoped for the same. That is why I did not admit to my secret, and why I kept writing. I wished to come to know you better, and I thought if I revealed myself too soon…" He squeezed his eyes shut and released a deep sigh.

"What did you think would happen?" she asked, her voice soft. "I would be upset?"

Though his laugh was short, and rather without humor, Griffin hastily looked up at her. "Are you not?"

"I am most upset." She took another step nearer. They were almost within touching distance, if he were to raise his hand. "Or I was. I find myself more curious now. When I met you near the flower girl, were you there for our exchange of letters?" Her eyes were narrowed, her focus intent upon him.

Curious was far better than angry, which was likely what he deserved.

"That was why I was there. To leave a letter, or retrieve one, but I also hoped each time that I might be fortunate enough to meet *you* there." He wanted to close the remaining distance between them himself, but he rather doubted he should.

Color entered her cheeks, giving them a rosy hue he found charming. "And that list of eligible gentlemen you provided to me. You included your own name. Why? Did you mean to use your letters to persuade me to give the men a chance?"

He swallowed, then nodded. "I did not intend to do it —not until the night of the ball. When we danced, and I had to introduce you to others, I knew I wanted a chance of my own." He lowered his gaze again, wondering exactly how pitiful he must sound to her.

Phoebe moved closer, her riding boots coming into view. "What sort of chance, Griffin?" His head jerked up at her use of his given name, and then he saw it—a sparkle in her eyes. His heart lightened with hope.

"A chance to come to know you, to court you." Finally, he raised his hand toward her, palm up. "To see if, perhaps, we suit one another as well as I feel we must."

She regarded his expression carefully, then looked down at his gloved hand. Slowly, she reached out to him, placing her hand in his. Everything in him both relaxed and became electrified at her touch. He sensed her understanding, her forgiveness, and something more. Something quite beautiful.

"I told a very close friend about you. About both my letter-writer and you, Griffin Fenwick." She looked up at him from beneath the brim of her hat. "She said I ought to meet my anonymous friend. She said, in fact, that the moment I laid eyes upon him I would know if I could care for him. You see, your letters made me curious. Then they rather enchanted me."

Griffin leaned closer, his eyes upon hers. "And? Now that you have laid eyes upon me?"

Her smile grew. She tipped her chin up bravely. "Griffin. I find I rather adore you, and if you do not ask to call upon me, if you do not seek my brother out and inquire after a courtship, I will be grievously disappointed." For a moment, her eyes glimmered with worry.

Griffin pulled in a sharp breath of air. "Phoebe, my dearest, most lovely friend. I rather intend to do more than court you. In fact, if you will permit me, I should rather like to kiss you."

A grin burst upon her beautiful face. Phoebe stood upon her toes, tilting her face toward his. They met in what little space remained between them, heedless of anyone watching, and sealing their fate, rather happily. Her lips were soft, sweet, and his free hand slid around her waist, pulling her closer. He had longed to kiss her since the night of the play; it was better than even his dreams. Everything felt warm, and right, and Griffin knew in the instant their lips touched that he would spend the rest of his life craving Phoebe's kisses.

When they parted, her hat tipped back rather perilously after their kiss, Griffin kept her close. "A courtship is all well and good, my love. But it will be terribly short."

Her already pink cheeks darkened, and her eyes gleamed. "I find I do not mind that idea. My dearest friend." Then she laughed. "To think, I owe my present happiness to your horrid duel in the park."

He joined in her laughter and remained with her in the park, walking hand-in-hand, a rather confused groom walking several paces behind, until it began to rain.

EPILOGUE
LETTER TO A FRIEND

To My Dear Daphne,

I have the most wonderful news to share. I am engaged to be married to Mr. Griffin Fenwick, the very gentleman we discussed less than a fortnight ago. He is everything I could wish for in a husband, attentive, kind, witty, and deeply in love with me. You must know how I have always had a plan, mapped out my life to suit what I thought best. I certainly never planned on falling in love with someone as spontaneous and ridiculous as my darling Griffin.

You may, perhaps, wonder what happened to my mysterious friend. You will never guess! Griffin and the anonymous friend are the same person. I will tell you all about it when next we meet. I hope it will be soon. If you are still in London in a fortnight, I hope you will attend the wedding ceremony. I have written our other friends to let them know, and have invited them to come if they are able.

Daphne, I do hope you are well. I could tell there was something on your mind when last we met. I have a feeling you might need the bracelet. Not that I think it is especially lucky or any such thing. But I cannot deny that having it these past weeks has given *me a measure of comfort and courage as I remembered you and the other girls.*

When I see you at my wedding, the bracelet will be yours.

I wish you well with all my heart.

Yours Most Sincerely,

Phoebe Kimball

Did you enjoy reading about Phoebe? There is more to the story of the five friends and their lucky bracelet. Continue with Daphne's story, **Romancing Her Rival**, *written by Joanna Barker.*

If you enjoyed Sally Britton's writing, turn the page for a list of her Regency titles.

ACKNOWLEDGMENTS & NOTES

This is the second series I've written with my dear friends and critique group. It isn't easy to put these books together, to work with one another to make certain we capture the voices of each other's characters, and it takes a certain amount of trust and patience. I'm grateful to know the women I work with on a personal level. A day never passes without one of us messaging the group. In the two years we've known each other, we've laughed and cried together, shared both triumph and heartache, and we've even lost our tempers. We get through it all, we remain friends, because there's something special holding us together.

Knowing these women in this way made our decision to write a second series together natural. We wanted to write about a group of friends, and as we worked together on the first scene of five girls, we laughed and giggled as much as our characters did. I hope you enjoy our stories of friendship as you continue through the series.

I'm also grateful for the other friends I have made while working in the world of words: my designer and dear friend Shaela Kay, my sweet editor Jenny Proctor, my proofreader and assistant Carri Flores, have all contributed to this book in one way or another.

Now for my usual caveat. Writing isn't easy. No matter how hard an author tries, they can never be perfect. I have yet to publish a book completely devoid of typos or minor mistakes - even the largest publishing houses in the world usually have what they call "an acceptable error rate." No book is perfect, because no author, editor, or proofreader is perfect, either. So I am all the more grateful for the wonderful people on my team who help me polish my drafts until they shine.

ALSO BY SALLY BRITTON

Heart's of Arizona Series:

Book #1, *Silver Dollar Duke*

The Inglewood Series:

Book #1, *Rescuing Lord Inglewood*

Book #2, *Discovering Grace*

Book #3, *Saving Miss Everly*

Book #4, *Engaging Sir Isaac*

Book #5, *Reforming Lord Neil*

The Branches of Love Series:

Prequel Novella, *Martha's Patience*

Book #1, *The Social Tutor*

Book #2, *The Gentleman Physician*

Book #3, *His Bluestocking Bride*

Book #4, *The Earl and His Lady*

Book #5, *Miss Devon's Choice*

Book #6, *Courting the Vicar's Daughter*

Book #7, *Penny's Yuletide Wish (A Novella)*

Stand Alone Romances:

The Captain and Miss Winter

His Unexpected Heiress

A Haunting at Havenwood

Timeless Romance Collection:

An Evening at Almack's, Regency Collection 12

ABOUT THE AUTHOR

Sally Britton, along with her husband and four incredible children, now live in Oklahoma. So far, they really like it there, even if the family will always consider Texas home.

Sally started writing her first story on her mother's electric typewriter, when she was fourteen years old. Reading her way through Jane Austen, Louisa May Alcott, and Lucy Maud Montgomery, Sally decided to write about the elegant, complex world of centuries past.

Sally graduated from Brigham Young University in 2007 with a bachelor's in English, her emphasis on British literature. She met and married her husband not long after and they've been building their happily ever after since that day.

Vincent Van Gogh is attributed with the quote, "What is done in love is done well." Sally has taken that as her motto, for herself and her characters, writing stories where love is a choice.

All of Sally's published works are available on Amazon.com and you can connect with Sally and sign up for her newsletter on her website, AuthorSallyBritton.com.

Made in the USA
Monee, IL
18 January 2024

51999392R00079